Nancy Drew®
in
The Witch Tree Symbol

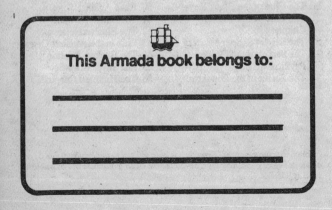

This Armada book belongs to:

Other Nancy Drew Mystery Stories ® in Armada

* For contractural reasons, Armada has been obliged to publish from No. 51 onwards before publishing Nos. 36–50. These missing numbers will be published as soon as possible.

The Nancy Drew Mystery Stories®

The Witch Tree Symbol

Carolyn Keene

Armada

First published in the U.K. in 1974 by
William Collins Sons & Co. Ltd., London and Glasgow.
First published in Armada in 1985 by
Fontana Paperbacks,
8 Grafton Street, London W1X 3LA.

Printed and bound in Great Britain by
William Collins Sons & Co. Ltd.

CONTENTS

"If you like it, buy it. The table's not so expensive,"
Mr. Zinn answered.

·1·

A Mysterious Intruder

"I wouldn't go into that spooky old house alone for anything," declared the plump, nervous woman who sat beside Nancy Drew in the blue convertible.

Nancy, a slender, attractive girl of eighteen, smiled as she turned the car into the winding, tree-shaded driveway of the Follett mansion. "Why, Mrs Tenney," she said, "your great-aunt lived here alone for a great many years and was perfectly safe."

"She was just lucky not to have had burglars," Mrs Tenney replied. "Aunt Sara was so absentminded that most of the time she didn't know what was going on. But one thing she did keep track of was the beautiful antique furniture in her library. She never used the room, but wouldn't part with a piece of the furniture in it."

As Nancy parked the car in front of the faded green Victorian house, she remarked, "Everything looks peaceful. Shall we go in?"

Mrs Tenney gazed cautiously at the closed curtains, then said, "I suppose we must. After all, that's why I asked you to come. Oh, Nancy," the woman seemed to overcome her nervousness as she rambled on, "wait until you see the furniture. Especially the two matching cherry tables that George Washington once used. They're priceless. And to think that I've inherited one half of everything in this house!"

Nancy and her companion alighted. Mrs Tenney produced a key and opened the door. Snapping on a light, she led the way into a large hall on each side of which were arched entranceways to various rooms. Nancy followed her to the second archway on the right. At the entrance to the library, Mrs Tenney came to an abrupt stop and gasped.

"What's the matter?" Nancy asked quickly.

"They're gone! All the valuable antiques!" Mrs Tenney cried out.

She hurried frantically into the library, paused, and pointed. "There's where a fine old sofa stood," she said. "And at each end of it was one of the tables I told you about."

Mrs Tenney began to weep, then, as a sudden thought struck her, she stopped and said, "So! Well, he won't get away with this!"

The titian-haired, blue-eyed girl waited for the woman to explain her statement. Nancy had met Mrs Tenney only a short time ago and felt that it would be presumptuous to question her at the moment. The woman had only recently moved into the neighbourhood where Nancy lived. Having heard of the young detective as being courageous and level-headed, she had asked Nancy to accompany her to the dreary Follett mansion, since she did not want to be alone in the house while she took an inventory of the furnishings recently willed to her.

"My cousin!" she burst out. "My second cousin, Alpha Zinn! He came here and took the best pieces before I had a chance to decide on what I wanted!"

Nancy ventured a question. "Was Mr Zinn bequeathed the other half of the contents of this house?"

"Yes. We have never been friends. I don't trust him. He's an antique dealer and a sharp trader."

Nancy did not feel that these were very valid reasons for her accusations, especially when half the furniture belonged to Zinn anyway. "Perhaps it was someone else," she suggested. "Let's look for a clue to the burglar."

She began searching carefully. In a corner of the library Nancy picked up a small, crumpled piece of paper. Drawn on it, in coloured crayon, was a white-rimmed circle with a red centre in which was a black star. Printed underneath the circle were the words: WITCH TREE SYMBOL.

"How very strange!" Nancy thought, as she walked across the room to show it to Mrs Tenney. "Do you know what this is?" she asked.

The woman gave the drawing one glance, then said, "Of course. It's a Pennsylvania Dutch hex sign. Well, I guess that's all the proof we need," she stated flatly. "Alpha Zinn lives up in that part of Pennsylvania. I just know he was here and took every stick of good furniture. Not only his, but mine!"

Nancy had to admit that under the circumstances Mr Zinn was a logical suspect, but she was far from being completely convinced of his guilt. "What does 'witch tree symbol' mean?" she asked.

"I don't know," Mrs Tenney replied. "But what difference does that make when I know Alpha is guilty?"

Although Nancy felt sure that the hex sign might be the clue to solving the mystery she did not say so. Whether Mrs Tenney's cousin or someone else were the real culprit, he very likely had come from the area where quaint hex designs, originated in the days of witchcraft, are sometimes painted on barns. Nancy questioned Mrs Tenney further about the hex sign. But the woman could throw no light on the strange symbol's significance.

"When were you in this house last?" Nancy asked.

"About a week ago. I came here with one of the executors," Mrs Tenney replied. "He gave me a key and said I might come back any time I wished."

Mrs Tenney went on to say that the executor had left and she had stayed behind to inspect some of the furnishings upstairs. But she had begun to feel uneasy alone in the old mansion and had decided to leave.

"Are you sure you locked the front door?" Nancy asked.

Mrs Tenney became lost in thought for a few moments.

She frowned, and then said, "I'm sure that man locked the door after us."

"What man?" Nancy inquired. "I thought you said the executor had already left."

"Oh, it wasn't the executor," Mrs Tenney answered quickly. "It was the antique dealer."

Nancy sighed to herself. The woman certainly was giving a confused account of things! But patiently she urged Mrs Tenney to tell the whole story.

"Well, this is the way it happened that day," the woman replied. "I was just going to lock the door when a nice-looking man drove up here. He said that he had heard about Mrs Follett's collection, and was interested in buying any articles that her heirs did not want; so I took him into the library for a quick look. When we came out I gave him the key to lock the door."

"I see," said Nancy, thinking how easy it would have been for the man to make a pretence of locking it. "Please go on."

"The man said he had read about Aunt Sara's antiques in a newspaper. He was in River Heights on business and decided to drive over here and take a look at the pieces."

"Then he wasn't a local dealer," Nancy commented thoughtfully. "Where did this man come from?"

"I don't know." Mrs Tenney shrugged. "But he was staying at a hotel in town."

Nancy pondered this information for a full minute. Then she said that there was a good possibility this man might be the furniture thief and should be investigated at once.

"At which hotel was he staying?" she asked.

Mrs Tenney flushed with embarrassment, admitting that she could not remember, nor could she recall his name.

"It doesn't matter," said Nancy. "We can go to each hotel in town and inquire about guests interested in antique furniture."

As Nancy finished speaking, she and Mrs Tenney became aware of light footsteps overhead. Someone was on the first floor! Mrs Tenney stood frozen to the spot, every bit of colour draining from her face. But without a moment's hesitation Nancy dashed out to the stairway and started up the steps.

"Oh, don't go up there!" Mrs Tenney gasped. "You might get hurt!"

Nancy stopped, not because of the warning, but because she heard stairs creaking. The intruder was probably scurrying to escape!

"Is there a back stairway?" Nancy asked Mrs Tenney. Not receiving an answer, she whirled round.

To her dismay, Mrs Tenney lay on the floor in a faint. Nancy, although realizing that the intruder might get away, rushed to give the woman first aid. A few moments later Mrs Tenney's eyelids flickered open. Instantly Nancy got to her feet and again dashed off in pursuit of the intruder.

But the pause had proved to be costly. When she reached the back of the old mansion, Nancy found the outside kitchen door open. Looking out, she saw a tall, slender man disappearing through a hedge at the rear of the property.

Realizing that it would be useless to try to overtake him, Nancy locked the back door and returned to Mrs Tenney. The woman was sitting on the staircase.

"How do you feel?" Nancy asked her.

"Oh, terrible, just terrible," Mrs Tenney moaned. "Please drive me home."

"Right away." Nancy locked the front door and helped the woman into the car. On the way to Mrs Tenney's house, Nancy asked for a full description of the antique dealer. Although the woman was almost too distraught to talk, Nancy learned that he was tall, slender, and dark, with flashing eyes and was soft-spoken.

"But I'm sure that *he's* not the thief," Mrs Tenney insisted, as Nancy pulled up in front of her home. "I still think that cousin of mine is responsible—Aunt Sara always said he kept an eagle eye on her antiques. Of course, I'd hate to have him know I'm suspicious of him. But I'd certainly like to know if I'm right." Then, as a sudden thought struck Mrs Tenney, she added, "Nancy, would you like to take this case for me? I know you're a good detective. Go up to see Alpha Zinn and find out whether he took the antiques."

Nancy promised that she would think it over and let the woman know. Right now, she intended to drive into town and find out about the mysterious antique dealer who was staying in River Heights.

"By the way," asked Nancy, "what does your cousin look like?"

"Oh, he's short and plump," replied Mrs Tenney. "He eats too much."

Mrs Tenney got out of the car and Nancy hurried off on her search. Starting with the largest, Nancy went from hotel to hotel. As she did, she told herself that if her hunch were right, the suspect would have had plenty of time to check out and escape.

Finally she came to the Pickwick Arms and repeated her query: Was a tall, slender, dark-haired, soft-spoken man registered there? Nancy added that she did not know his name, but wanted to get in touch with him about some antique furniture which he had already examined.

The receptionist smiled and said, "I guess you mean Mr Hoelt. Mr Roger Hoelt. I'm sorry, miss, but you're too late. He rushed in here, packed in a hurry, and checked out about fifteen minutes ago!"

·2·

Plans for Sleuthing

The suspect had left the hotel in a hurry! This certainly implied guilt.

"Did Mr Hoelt leave a forwarding address?" Nancy asked the hotel receptionist.

"Sorry. He didn't, and I have no idea where he was going," the man replied. "But perhaps you might find him in the New York City telephone directory. He gave that as his business address."

Since this did not tie in with her surmise that the antique dealer had dropped the paper with the hex symbol, and therefore had come from Pennsylvania Dutch country, Nancy felt that perhaps she was following a false clue.

But then another idea occurred to her. Deciding to take the receptionist into her confidence, she identified herself and said that Mr Hoelt was a suspect in a questionable business deal.

"Could you give me some information that might be helpful in locating Mr Hoelt?" she asked. "Perhaps he made some long-distance telephone calls."

"I'll look up his bill," the man offered, and disappeared into the office for a few minutes. Then he came back and said, "Mr Hoelt made a long-distance call to Lancaster, Pennsylvania, three days ago. I remember now that he was very insistent that we put the call in at exactly three p.m. He talked for a long time according to the amount of the bill. Will that help you?"

Nancy's heart was beating faster. Maybe this was not a

false clue after all! Lancaster was in Pennsylvania Dutch country! "Thank you very much," she said, smiling. "Have you a record of the number he called?"

The receptionist went into the office again. When he returned a few minutes later he had discouraging news. "I checked the number called and find it was a call box in Lancaster, so I'm afraid that won't help you."

As she left the Pickwick Arms, Nancy's eyes were bright with excitement. She was never happier than when working on a new mystery. From the time she was asked to help solve *The Secret of Shadow Ranch* up to the recent and hazardous *Clue in the Old Album*, the young amateur detective had never been discouraged by an elusive suspect.

Now, as she thought about Roger Hoelt, she was more convinced than ever that he had stolen the valuable antiques from the Follett mansion. Since the furniture must have been taken out of the house a day or two earlier, perhaps Hoelt had made his call to Pennsylvania to arrange with a friend to pick it up in a truck. Wondering how to find him, Nancy thought, "He may be listed in the police files. I'll ask Chief McGinnis."

The River Heights police captain, an old friend of Nancy's, greeted her warmly as she walked into headquarters. "I'm sure this call isn't just for sociable reasons," he said, a twinkle in his eye. "Out with it, Nancy. What is it this time? Another mystery?"

"Now stop teasing," said Nancy, blushing a little. "I suppose if you couldn't guess that, you wouldn't be such a good police officer. Yes, I am working on another mystery. And I need some information. Have you a Roger Hoelt on your records?" Nancy explained that Hoelt did not live in the area and that he had given his address as New York City.

Chief McGinnis arose and went to a filing cabinet. Quickly he riffled through a series of cards.

"Here it is, Nancy," he said a moment later. "Roger Hoelt, six feet, slender, dark. Eyes brown, nose pointed, slight scar on tip of chin. Soft-spoken. Lived as child in Lancaster, Pennsylvania. Well, Nancy, is that your man?"

"That surely sounds like him."

The chief chuckled. "Why are you after Hoelt? Did he rob you of some jewellery?"

Nancy countered with, "Is that what Hoelt is—a jewel thief?"

Chief McGinnis nodded, becoming serious. "He was in prison for several years, serving time for holding up jewellery shops. In fact, the man made quite a haul right here in River Heights. Want to see his picture?"

"Yes, I'd better," Nancy replied. "I may need to know what he looks like."

After clearly implanting the man's face in her mind, Nancy told the chief about her suspicions in regard to the antique furniture missing from the Follett mansion. "Has it been reported to you yet?" she asked.

"No."

"Poor Mrs Tenney was so upset that I guess she forgot to notify you," said Nancy. "Suppose I give her a ring and have you talk to her."

Chief McGinnis handed Nancy his phone and she made the call. The chief then spoke to Mrs Tenney and promised to send two of his men out to the Follett house at once. He advised Mrs Tenney to get in touch with the executors immediately.

"Have one of them bring me a complete list of the missing articles," he directed.

After the chief put down the phone he turned to Nancy and gave her a broad smile. "I have a feeling that you, too, are going to hunt for this Roger Hoelt. I'd like to bet right now that you'll probably find him first." He chuckled.

The young sleuth was embarrassed. "You flatter me," she said. "The only reason I might find him before you do is because he's no longer in the River Heights vicinity. If I can arrange a trip, I'm going up to the Lancaster section of Pennsylvania and see if I can locate the missing furniture and the person who took it."

"Great idea," said Chief McGinnis. Then, as his phone rang, he waved goodbye, saying, "Best of luck to you, Nancy!"

At home Nancy was affectionately greeted by Hannah Gruen, the Drews' housekeeper. Plump and motherly, Hannah had lived with the family since Mrs Drew's death when Nancy was three.

"Nancy," the housekeeper said, "don't you ever get hungry? You were supposed to be here for a six-o'clock dinner and now it's half past seven."

Nancy gave Hannah a hug and apologized. "Now that you mention food, I'm starved." She grinned. "Let's eat!"

As they sat down to the dining-room table, Mrs Gruen complained good-naturedly that she never knew when the young detective and her lawyer father were going to show up for meals. Just then a car pulled into the driveway.

"It's Dad!" Nancy's face glowed as Mr Drew, a tall, handsome man, hurried into the house. A few moments later he joined them at the table.

"Mm-mm," he said. "Old-fashioned, home-made chicken soup!" He winked at Nancy. "Hannah must have known I'd be here in time for one of my favourite dishes."

Nancy laughed. "And you're here in time for another favourite dish of yours—a new mystery."

During the rest of the delicious meal of roast beef, with apple pie for dessert, Nancy told the others of the mystery which she had stumbled into that afternoon.

"Mrs Tenney wants me to go to the Pennsylvania Dutch country and see if her cousin is the one who removed the antiques from the Follett home," she said. "Personally, I'm sure he didn't and that it was Roger Hoelt."

From her bag Nancy took out the paper bearing the

strange hex symbol and showed it to her father and Mrs Gruen.

"I'm certain this is a good clue to the thief," she stated, "and that he came back to the old mansion to find it. Unfortunately for him, I picked it up first. But what does it mean?"

Mr Drew was also puzzled about the hex sign, but said he thought Nancy's reasoning was correct. He, too, felt that a trip into the Pennsylvania Dutch section would be a very interesting one for his daughter.

"Why don't you see if Bess and George can go with you?" he suggested, referring to two girls who were Nancy's close friends.

"That's a grand idea, Dad!" his daughter exclaimed enthusiastically.

As soon as the family finished eating, Nancy went to the phone and called each of the girls, who were cousins. Both George Fayne and Bess Marvin, eager to make the trip with her, received their parents' permission.

"When do we start?" asked George, who was as boyish in her manner as her name indicated.

"We may as well leave tomorrow morning," said Nancy. "I'll call Bess back and tell her to be ready by ten o'clock. Can you make it then?"

"Sure," replied George. "I can pack in a jiffy."

Nancy made the call to Bess, then went to the kitchen to help Hannah with the dishes. "Where's Togo?" she asked. Togo was her small dog. The frisky fox terrier was usually underfoot at dinnertime, begging for an extra meal.

"Oh, I let him out just before you came home," said Hannah. "Togo will probably race around the neighbourhood for a couple of hours before he's ready to return home."

Nancy did not approve of her pet roaming the streets, but she did not want to hurt the housekeeper's feelings and therefore made no comment.

Hannah Gruen changed the subject. "There's just one thing that bothers me about your taking on this case," she remarked. "This hex business."

"Oh, that's an old-fashioned belief," Nancy said, smiling. "People today don't believe in witchcraft, and the hex signs that were once used to ward off the witches are now only decorations on barns."

The housekeeper was not convinced. "I've heard some pretty frightening stories about people being hexed," she declared sombrely. "I certainly wouldn't want anything like that to happen to you."

Nancy put an arm round Hannah's shoulders. "Now don't you worry," she said soothingly.

After the dishes were washed, Nancy decided to go outside and look for Togo. As she stood on the sidewalk whistling to her pet and calling his name, she noticed a car driving slowly by. The only occupant was the driver, but it was too dark for Nancy to see his face. He went on and once more she called Togo's name. Still the terrier did not respond and Nancy began to worry about him.

Looking up the street, she noted that the car had made a wide turn at the corner and was coming back. Was the driver waiting for someone to come out of a house? Nancy wondered.

At this moment Togo appeared on the opposite sidewalk. Nancy called to the dog to wait until the car had gone by. But the little terrier, eager to come to his mistress, made a dash across the street.

The driver of the car, instead of slowing down, suddenly put on a burst of speed and headed directly for Togo. The terrified dog tried to avoid the car, but it swerved and sped towards him.

The next moment Togo gave a yelp of pain. The car had hit him!

·3·

"Chust for Pretty"

"Togo!" Nancy cried fearfully, as the terrier was thrown to the side of the street. The car that had struck the dog flashed past. Nancy ran to her pet, who was alternately whining pitifully and giving short yelps of pain. She was alarmed that he might have been fatally injured.

"Oh, you poor little thing!" she murmured tenderly, wondering what she might do to relieve the dog's suffering.

Leaning over to pick him up, she noticed a long cut on the terrier's hip, but there were no other marks. Suddenly Togo stood up and shook himself. Nancy's heart leaped with joy. Her beloved pet was going to be all right!

Gently she lifted the dog and carried him inside to the kitchen, where she bathed the cut with antiseptic. He nosed her hand gratefully, then started to lick the wound himself.

Hannah, who had dashed down from the first floor, looked on in mingled dismay and bewilderment. Nancy explained what had happened.

"That man in the car deliberately tried to kill Togo!" she said angrily. "I was so worried about him I forgot to look at the licence number on the car."

"I'm sorry you didn't!" Hannah replied vehemently, going into a tirade about hit-and-run drivers. "And I told you, Nancy," she reminded the girl, "that hex signs bring trouble! That man in the car hexed Togo for sure!"

Nancy tried to calm the excited housekeeper. "That is not possible," she said.

"Oh, yes, it is!" Mrs Gruen insisted. "It all ties in!"

21

Her reasoning was that the man in the car was the same one whom Nancy had surprised at the Follett mansion and reported to the police. "He's hexed you too—put a spell on you."

"But, Hannah, that's wishing bad luck on someone, not causing it, as he did."

The housekeeper declared that it made no difference how it happened. So long as Nancy worked on the case, the suspect would try to harm her.

"I think you'd better give up the Lancaster trip."

"Why, Hannah, I couldn't do that," Nancy protested. "And anyway, if he's here and I'm in Pennsylvania, I'll be safer," she teased. "Besides, I want a chance to practise my German!"

The woman was adamant. "Let the police catch the furniture thief," she said. "There's something queer about that witch tree symbol. I don't like it."

Mr Drew, who had been talking on the upstairs telephone, now came to join them. He was relieved to learn that Togo was all right. At once Hannah told him about her worries concerning Nancy, but the lawyer did not share her point of view.

"As to the hex business, we are intelligent people and don't believe in witchcraft. If Nancy is careful, I think it will be safe for her to make the trip."

Later that evening Nancy packed a suitcase and, before retiring, exchanged goodbyes with her father, since he was leaving early in the morning for an out-of-town case. Nancy promised to let him know of any progress she made and where she would be staying.

After breakfast the next morning, Nancy took her car to a local garage for a check-up. When she returned home, Hannah Gruen met her at the door. In her hand was a special-delivery letter which had come for Nancy.

"I'm sure this means trouble," the housekeeper said gloomily.

The letter had been mailed from Montville, a town about twenty miles from River Heights. Nancy quickly tore open the envelope and pulled out a single sheet of paper. On it was the strange hex symbol! The words "witch tree symbol" were missing but underneath, printed in a bold hand, was the warning: STAY HOME!

"Now I hope you're convinced," said Hannah. "If you do go to Lancaster, you'll be taking your life in your hands!"

Instead of being worried, Nancy was more intrigued than ever at the prospect of making the trip. Montville was on the way to Lancaster! The furniture thief had already started for Pennsylvania Dutch country!

To Hannah the girl detective said, "I admit that the sender of this note is trying to scare me off the case. But he's not going to do it!" Giving the woman a resounding kiss, Nancy added, "I'll be very, very careful. Please don't worry."

"I can't promise that," the housekeeper answered. "I'll worry about you every minute until you're back, safe and sound." She sighed. "But since you're determined to go, I'll hold good thoughts for you. Have a nice time, dear, and drive carefully."

Nancy gathered up her suitcase, coat, and a lunch the housekeeper had packed, and carried them to the blue convertible. After waving to Hannah and throwing her a kiss from the car window, she backed into the street and headed for Bess Marvin's home.

Bess, blonde-haired, blue-eyed, and pretty, though slightly overweight, stood on the porch waiting. She hurried down the walk, tossed her bag into the rear of the car, and climbed in beside Nancy.

"Hello!" she said. "Sounds like an exciting trip. I've been reading up on the Pennsylvania Dutch country. What a place to eat! Best food in the whole United States!"

Nancy laughed. Though Bess was sometimes less courageous than either Nancy or George when working on mysteries, she was never timid about trying new foods. She was a gay companion and loyal friend, and could be depended upon for help in a real emergency.

A few minutes later they picked up George Fayne, who wore a fitted white blouse and a white and brown skirt. Over her arm George carried a matching jacket. The tomboyish girl, after putting her suitcase in the back, jumped into the front seat with a "Hi there!" and slammed the door. "It's a grand day, eh? I like August weather. It's good for sports—not too hot and not too cold."

Her cousin Bess sniffed and remarked that so far August had been too hot for comfort. Nancy laughingly warned the cousins not to start even friendly arguments so early in the morning. "I'd call this a perfect day to begin solving our mystery," she declared gaily.

"Please. tell us everything about it," Bess begged. "You were pretty vague on the phone. I hope that it's not too dangerous a one," she added.

As they drove along, Nancy told the entire story. The two girls listened intently, knowing that if they were to be of assistance to Nancy, they would need to know all that had happened so far. Bess remarked that she did not like the hex symbol angle of the mystery. She was inclined to agree with Hannah Gruen that it might bring bad luck to Nancy.

The young sleuth assured Bess that she did not believe in the superstition. "Nor in ghosts, zombies, or witchcraft," she said with a chuckle. "But," she continued, growing serious, "I understand there are some people in the back country of Pennsylvania who still think it's possible to hex people. Of course, most of the farmers just laugh at this nowadays."

Several hours later the girls reached the area where the first hex.signs appeared on barns. They stopped to admire several, and even Bess had to admit that the various circular designs, using motifs of birds, stars, and crosses, were very colourful and attractive. Seeing a farmer coming from one of the larger red barns, Nancy stopped the car and asked him the designs' true significance.

Smiling, the burly man replied, "It's chust for pretty."

"And has nothing to do with any superstition?" Bess asked.

The man shook his head. "No. Chust to make pretty the barn. But queer folks think it is for to chase witches. That is foolish, ain't?"

The girls nodded and drove on.

George smiled. "I could hardly figure out that man's quaint language. We may find ourselves having some trouble up here understanding what people say."

"Yes," Nancy agreed. "And I think if we don't understand, we'd better ask."

The girls rode for nearly an hour through the methodically planned, beautiful farm country, stopping only long enough to eat lunch. Everything looked spick-and-span. Fields of corn, potatoes, and tobacco were straight and green. Weedless vegetable gardens of beets, carrots, and beans were surrounded by neat borders of flowers. Cockscomb, begonia, and geranium bloomed in profusion.

"These are the finest-looking farms I've ever seen," Bess remarked presently. "What fun it would be to live on one!"

Nancy said her father had told her of the various divisions of the Pennsylvania Dutch country. Around the Lancaster area were most of the plain people. "The owners of the farms there take great pride in their land," Nancy went on. "They attribute their abundant harvests to deep ploughing, correct rotation of crops, fertilizer, and plenty of hard work."

"Which section is Mr Alpha Zinn's home in?"

"Beyond Lancaster, in the part where the Amish live."

"Amish?" Bess repeated. "Tell us about them."

Nancy said that Mrs Tenney had explained to her that there were two types of Amish, the Church Amish, who are comparatively modern and own cars and electrical appliances; and the House Amish, who are very strict and do not believe in using any of these "fancy" things. "They feel that hard work with the hands is much better for the health and the soul," Nancy concluded.

After a while she stopped and consulted a map. Then she said, "I think this is the side road that leads to Mr Zinn's farmhouse. Mrs Tenney gave me general directions."

Nancy drove on, watching road signs carefully. Presently she turned on to a bisecting road and drove a little faster. She had not gone more than a quarter of a mile when the car began to chug peculiarly and started to slow down.

"That's funny," Nancy said, frowning, and the other girls looked worried too.

They glanced quickly at the various dials on the dashboard. There was plenty of petrol, the oil gauge was registering pressure, and the car was not heating up.

"I wonder what is wrong," George remarked.

"I don't know," said Nancy. "But the engine's not taking any petrol."

The engine suddenly died, and the car, after rolling a few feet, stopped.

The three girls looked around in dismay. There was not a house in sight and the next town where there was likely to be a garage was several miles away.

Nancy got out, raised the bonnet of the car, and looked for loose or broken wires. She could find none and finally shook her head.

"We're really stuck!" she announced.

·4·

The Runaway Girl

Bess and George, who had jumped out of the car to join Nancy, looked down into the engine of the stalled convertible.

"The hex is already working," Bess remarked. "Now a spell has been put on our car."

Nancy laughed. "I can almost believe you, Bess. But I shan't let it work long."

"I wonder if we could get help at the next farm," Bess suggested.

"If it happens to be a House Amish family," said Nancy, "they won't know anything about cars."

"I suppose the best thing to do," George spoke up, "is to wait for a car to come along and give one of us a lift into town to find a mechanic."

Ten minutes went by, but no vehicle came along the side road. Bess had climbed back into the car and was studying a map. George, who was looking in the direction from which they had come, suddenly called out:

"Here comes someone!"

The others glanced back. An Amish woman, wearing a black dress which reached to the top of her shoes, a black bonnet, and a white shawl and apron, walked slowly towards them.

"She must live nearby," said Bess, "and will know some-. one who can help us."

To the girls' surprise, as the woman came closer, they could see that she was very young—probably no more than sixteen years old.

27

Nancy stepped forward. She waited for the Amish girl to greet her, but she merely nodded to the group, a faraway look in her eyes, and walked on.

George glanced at Nancy, whispering, "That's odd. Country folks are usually very friendly."

"Maybe it's the custom here for outsiders to speak first," thought Nancy, and hurried after the girl.

"Hello," she said. "Our car won't run. Could you tell us where we might have it fixed?"

The Amish girl stopped and turned. She smiled gently at Nancy. She was very pretty, with large brown eyes and long lashes.

"I am so sorry about the car," she said. "You are visitors here, ain't?"

Nancy gave her name and added that she was from River Heights. She introduced Bess and George.

"I am Manda Kreutz," the girl told them. "I am walking from Lancaster."

"Lancaster?" George repeated. "That's over ten miles from here."

Manda nodded. "It is good to walk," she said, "and I know short cuts across the fields." Then her face clouded. "I am going back to my home, but my father—maybe he will not take me back."

The three girls from River Heights were startled by the announcement. They were curious to know what Manda Kreutz meant but did not want to embarrass her by asking for an explanation.

But apparently Manda suddenly decided that she could trust the three friendly girls and that they would understand her problem. Even though their way of living was far different from hers, they were not much older than she and shared the same feelings.

"We are Amish and my father is very strict," Manda said. "When I finished eighth grade, he wanted me to stay home and work on the farm. But I wanted to study more and learn about the world."

She had decided recently that perhaps this was wrong. Life was very good on an Amish farm and there was never any want.

"But I did not appreciate this," she said. "I ran away from home three months ago and went to Lancaster. In the daytime I worked in a bakery, and in the evenings I attended night school."

Wistfully she added, "But I miss my people. And yet I am so afraid my father will not let me live on the farm any more."

The three girls assured Manda that everything would probably work out and wished her the best of luck. Then Nancy asked her again if she knew anyone around who might repair the car.

"Yes," the Amish girl replied. "Rudolph—he is on a farm a mile from here—he can help you. He's Church Amish."

Manda offered to stop there and ask Rudolph to bring his tool kit. Nancy thanked her, but said she would walk along with Manda to talk to Rudolph herself. Nancy was intrigued by the girl and her story. Also, she was eager to learn more about the Amish people and their customs.

Manda seemed pleased by the arrangement. Bess and George said they would stay with the car until Nancy and the mechanic returned. As the Amish girl and Nancy hurried along the road, Manda talked freely about her problem.

"Papa is afraid if I learn too much I will not be an Amish woman any longer. But he is wrong. I might not be so strict as he is. We have no conveniences in our house or on our farm. I think that is foolish. Papa and Mama work too hard. And we have no books except our German Bible and the *Ga-brauch Buch*."

"What is the *Ga-brauch Buch*?" Nancy asked.

Manda explained that it told about powwowing—how to cure people when they are ill. "It is not done by medicine," she said. "It is accomplished by the 'laying on of hands' of the sick. Not everyone can learn this and make it work. My mother can powwow."

Again Nancy looked puzzled and Manda said that the "laying on of hands" was called powwowing. Then she added, "But I'd like to read and learn more things. I do not think this is wrong."

Presently a farmhouse came into sight and Manda said that was where Nancy would find Rudolph. "I will leave you now," the Amish girl said. "I hope Rudolph can fix your car all right."

"You still have a long way to walk," said Nancy. "Why don't you wait until the car is fixed and I'll drive you home?"

Manda's face took on a look of fright, then she said, "Oh, no! My father is strict House Amish and would never forgive me if I came home in a car. I thank you. I will walk the rest of the way."

Nancy said goodbye and watched the girl as she plodded down the road. Then, turning, she walked up the lane to Rudolph's house. A rosy-cheeked, red-haired young man, wearing a straight-brimmed black hat and black home-made cloth braces over his red shirt, saw her coming. He walked to meet Nancy and then bowed.

"I was told by Manda Kreutz that you are an expert mechanic," Nancy said. "My car is stuck down the road. Can you help me out?"

"*Ya*, I will help you," he said. "I will get my car and tools." He disappeared behind the house for a few minutes, then drove out a small car.

Nancy climbed in beside him and they went back to the stalled convertible where she introduced Bess and George. "Girls, this is Rudolph," she said.

The young man acknowledged the introduction with a nod of his head, then said to George, "You are a girl? Your name is George, ain't?"

George chuckled and admitted that was her name.

Rudolph shook his head and remarked that among plain people a man has a man's name and a woman a woman's name.

The tomboyish girl did not take offence at the criticism. Laughing, she told Rudolph that she had not named herself. "But I like having a boy's name," she admitted. "It's different."

Rudolph made no further comment. He began investigating the car and worked with amazing speed. One minute he was under the convertible, the next he was tinkering under the bonnet, and a moment later he was reaching in to the dashboard to test the ignition. Within five minutes, Rudolph said he had found the trouble.

"What is it?" Nancy asked.

"A connection wire—a twist in it." He soon had this fixed and the car started smoothly. As Nancy was paying Rudolph, she asked the young man whether he knew Alpha Zinn.

"*Ya*. He sells old furniture. It is not worth much but he charges a high price. That is not the way we Amish would do."

Rudolph said no more. Apparently he was a man of few words. Jumping into his car, he started the engine and drove down the road. Then the girls got into the convertible and started off.

Nancy glanced at her watch. "I'm afraid that it's too late now to call on Mr Zinn today."

Bess agreed and declared she was getting hungry, anyway. She would like to have one of those big Pennsylvania Dutch meals she had read about.

"So would I," said Nancy. "But first I'd like to go to the Kreutz farm and see how Manda made out. I have a feeling that if her father is as stern as she said he may not let her, stay. Then we can take her somewhere else. I'm sure she's dead tired."

"Good idea," said George. "Bess will have to wait."

The girls did not know exactly where the Kreutz farm was,

but would inquire farther down the road. There was a good chance, too, of overtaking Manda before she reached her home. But though they followed the road for three miles they did not see her.

"She probably took a short cut across the fields," George remarked.

Nancy pulled into the next farm to ask for directions. A serene-faced woman answered the door when George knocked. She wore a dainty white mull cap over her straight, tightly pulled-back black hair which was twisted into a bun at the nape of her neck. In reply to George's question, she pointed across the fields, saying, "At the next crossroad turn left and you can't miss the Kreutz farm."

Ten minutes later Nancy pulled up in front of the Kreutz homestead. It was a large, plain, two-storey house without blinds or curtains.

A short distance away was a very large stone barn built on two levels of ground. There were several other smaller buildings dotting the yards.

Since no one was around, Nancy got out and knocked on the front door. It was nearly half a minute before anyone answered. Then an Amish woman, who looked as if she had been crying, opened the door. Nancy was sure that things had not gone well for Manda.

"You're Mrs Kreutz?" Nancy asked, smiling.

The woman nodded but did not say anything. Nancy wondered if it was because she was shy or whether she might be too choked up to speak.

"Is Manda at home?" Nancy inquired.

"You know Manda?" the woman countered.

Nancy replied that she had met the girl on the road. Mrs Kreutz gave Nancy and the cousins, who were still in the car, searching looks, then said, "Manda did not say you were coming here."

Nancy told the whole story and suddenly Mrs Kreutz burst into tears. "Manda has gone again!" she wailed.

"Papa is so strict. He told Manda she could live here again, but he gave orders that nobody in the family would be allowed to speak to her."

"How dreadful!" Nancy cried involuntarily. "And you have a big family?"

"Six sons. They are married and have their own farms, but they visit us often. Papa and I do not agree about Manda," Mrs Kreutz went on, "but Papa is *mayschter*."

Noticing the girls' puzzled expressions, Mrs Kreutz said it meant "master" and whatever instructions Papa gave had to be obeyed.

Suddenly Mrs Kreutz looked pleadingly at Nancy. "Maybe Papa would listen to you, since you are outside our family. He will not admit to us, but his feelings are hurt because his only daughter has left home. Please talk to him about Manda. He is near the barn by the bull pens."

Nancy agreed to talk to him, although she had little hope of its doing any good. Bess and George got out of the car and the three girls walked towards the barn.

Behind it, they saw a large, fenced-in enclosure with three pens. In each stood a huge black bull.

Mr Kreutz was working in the first one. He was a giant of a man, with a ruddy complexion, sandy hair, and a long beard.

As he heard the girls' footsteps, the farmer looked up. At the same instant the huge bull beside him lowered its horns, caught up the man and threw him across the pen!

·5·

Nancy's Strategy

Bess screamed. This seemed to anger the bull. With a loud
snort he lowered his head as if to make a second attack on
Mr Kreutz, who lay stunned near the gate. Bess cried out
again. The animal delayed his charge momentarily, eyeing
the girl malevolently.

"Girls! Quick!" Nancy cried, seeing several buckets of
water standing by the barn wall. "George, grab one of
these!"

By now, Nancy had a pail in her hands. With full force
she threw the bucket of water over the fence at the bull's
head, just as he headed for the farmer again. The huge
animal stopped dead, temporarily blinded by the water.

Then his fury increased. Bellowing, he plunged towards
Mr Kreutz, who still lay motionless. As George threw her
pail of water at the animal with all her might, Nancy called
to Bess, "Stand by the gate and be ready to open it when I
tell you!" Nancy grabbed up another pail and heaved it into
the pen. Then, reaching through the bars, she grabbed
Mr Kreutz by his shirt and dragged him forward. The bull,
confused by the attack, backed away. Nancy took advantage
of the pause.

"Open the gate!" she said quickly.

As Bess did so, Nancy and George reached in and dragged
Mr Kreutz to safety. Bess then slammed the gate shut and
locked it.

With a roar the bull rammed headfirst into the bars of the
pen, trying to batter them down with his horns. Fortunately,

the bars were strongly built and he made little impression on the wood.

Looking round for more water, Nancy spied a water wheel in a sluiceway. Grabbing a pail, she dashed over, filled it, and hurried back to Mr Kreutz. Dipping her fresh handkerchief into the cold water, she applied it to his forehead. Bess massaged his wrists and presently the man opened his eyes. Luckily, he had not suffered any injury.

"*Wuu bin ich?*" the man murmured.

"You're with friends," Nancy replied to his question of where he was. "Just lie quietly for a little while and you'll be all right."

Mr Kreutz closed his eyes but half a minute later he opened them again. Sitting up, he gazed at the three girls. Then he heard the noise of the stamping bull and this seemed to recall to his mind what had happened.

"But how did I get out here?" he asked.

"We dragged you from the pen," George said bluntly. "If it hadn't been for the quick-wittedness of Nancy here"— she patted her chum on the shoulder—"you might have been killed by that awful bull."

"But where did you come from?" Mr Kreutz asked. "Oh, I remember now. I saw you just before the bull tossed me."

Nancy decided to wait until the farmer felt better before she mentioned Manda. The girls helped him to his feet, then assisted him to the house. Mrs Kreutz, looking from a window, saw them coming and hurried out the kitchen door.

"Oh, Papa, what is the matter?" she cried.

Her husband, still somewhat shaken, did not reply, so Bess explained.

"*Ach!*" Mrs Kreutz wrung her hands. "Poor Papa!"

"He'll be all right," Nancy hastened to assure her.

They all went into the kitchen and Mr Kreutz sat down in a wooden armchair. Conversation ceased as Mrs Kreutz went to the big black stove and ladled out steaming soup from a huge, old-fashioned kettle into a crockery bowl. Then, after handing this to her husband, she seated herself in another chair and motioned the girls to sit down also. Not a word was spoken as the man cupped the bowl in his hands and drank the soup.

"*Iss guut*," he said finally, setting the bowl on a table.

The girls, meanwhile, had been glancing round the large kitchen. One wall was completely taken up by a fireplace with its traditional Dutch oven set in one side of the stonework. Above it hung copper kettles of various sizes. In the centre of the fireplace was a long iron arm from which was suspended a caldron.

Beside the stove stood a box filled with logs and the girls assumed that the cooking was done over a wood fire. There was an old-fashioned sink on another wall, but no plumbing. Apparently all water was carried in from the sluiceway. The wide board floor was bare, but had been scrubbed until it shone.

"I feel better," Mr Kreutz announced as he finished the soup. "Now will you girls tell me your names and why you are here?"

"But first," Mrs Kreutz interrupted, "maybe we should give our visitors some dinner, Papa."

"Yes," he said. The farmer glanced at a wooden wall clock brightly decorated with designs in blue and red. "It's time for my dinner also. We will all eat," he said.

Nancy, Bess, and George accepted the invitation at once and offered to help Mrs Kreutz. The woman smiled and asked whether they ever did any cooking, baking, and house cleaning at home.

"Oh my, yes!" the three girls answered in unison.

In his chair they could hear Mr Kreutz grunt in satisfaction. Several times during the preparation of supper Mrs Kreutz remarked on the girls' efficiency.

Nancy laughed. "Perhaps that's because we're so hungry."

A short time later they sat down to eat. The long wooden

table in the kitchen, with benches on either side of it, was loaded with food. There were orange and yellow and white cheeses, red, purple, and white grape jams, a platter of huge slices of home-made bread, dishes of apple butter, stewed peaches, and cherries.

Also, there were pickled onions, sour cantaloupe, and corn relish. For a hot dish there was boiled pot pie, made of rabbit and fluffy two-inch squares of pastry.

Bowls of soup were set at the places. There was neither cloth nor mats. Mr Kreutz said grace, then, before putting his spoon into the soup, he asked:

"Where's Manda? You have no place set for her!"

There was complete silence. The farmer repeated his question. Still receiving no answer, Mr Kreutz roared, "Why can't you tell me? Where is Manda?"

In a low voice his wife replied, "She has gone away again."

Mr Kreutz set his lips tightly together and stared out the window. His food went untouched and the girls sat in silence.

"Eat your supper!" the man said abruptly. "This does not concern you."

Ordinarily the three visitors would have offered to leave at once but felt this might annoy the man even more. They began to eat, feeling very ill at ease.

Mrs Kreutz did not touch her meal either and there were tears in her eyes. Finally she said, "Papa, you were very lucky to have these nice girls come by and help you when the bull threw you."

"*Ya*, I was. *Donnk*," he gave his curt thanks.

Nancy said she was glad that they had arrived in time.

Bess, to ease the tension, giggled and said, "It was the closest I've ever been to a bull and I hope it's the last."

Presently the Kreutzes relaxed and began to eat their dinner. The girls were soon satisfied, though they had not sampled half of the various dishes on the table.

"You have city appetites," said Mrs Kreutz.

"I suppose we have," said George. "That is, all of us except Bess." The plump girl had just reached for a piece of cake.

"In Amish country we like a little flesh on our maidens," said Mr Kreutz.

After the meal was over, the three girls helped their hostess wash and dry the heavy, plain dishes which they had used. Then Nancy said they must be leaving and whispered to the woman:

"Do you think I should say anything to Mr Kreutz about Manda?"

"I will fix this," the farmer's wife said, apparently getting a sudden inspiration. She called across the room to her husband, "Papa, I would like it for these girls to stay all night with us."

Mr Kreutz nodded. "That will make our thanks for saving my life."

Mrs Kreutz turned to Nancy and whispered, "Talk to him about Manda. It will be all right."

She did not explain further what she meant, but Nancy guessed that once an Amish person makes a promise, he does not go back on it. No matter what happened, the girls would spend the night there.

Walking over to Mr Kreutz, Nancy seated herself beside him and broached the subject of Manda.

"Bess and George and I met your lovely daughter on the road this afternoon, Mr Kreutz. She was looking forward to coming home and being with her mother and father again."

The farmer shifted uneasily in his chair. Finally he said, "Manda is a very disobedient daughter. Amish people have rules. We do not expect our children to break them. From the time they are small, we teach them to fear God and to work. We do not need to go out into the world to make money. We have security right on our own farms.

"We ask nothing from anyone." Then proudly he added,

"Security for an Amish man is not money. It is his family, his religion, and his farm."

Nancy pondered this for a moment, then she commented, "You say part of your security is your family. Then wouldn't you be happier if all your family were together?"

Mr Kreutz looked down at the floor. He did not reply for a full minute. Then he looked directly into Nancy's eyes. "You are a very unusual girl," he said. "You are wise beyond your years. You have good sense."

Nancy waited breathlessly for him to go on. To her surprise he asked abruptly, "Why are you up here where the Amish live?"

Nancy told him about the stolen Follett furniture.

"I think the thief may possibly be around here," she said, and explained about finding the drawing of the hex sign on the floor of the old mansion.

"You are a nice girl," said Mr Kreutz. "But I cannot understand why your papa lets you do things like this. You should be home cooking and cleaning."

Bess and George felt that it was time for them to take a hand in the conversation. In glowing terms they told about all the good Nancy had accomplished in solving mysteries.

"Why, she's restored lots of people to their families," Bess said impetuously.

The farmer's eyes grew wide, then he closed them, as if he were battling with his own problem. In a few minutes he opened them and looked off into space. At last he turned to Nancy.

"I want Manda back," he said. "If you can find missing persons, bring my daughter home."

Nancy assured him that she would be happy to look for Manda. Secretly the young detective did not feel very confident about locating the runaway. She had a feeling that this time Manda had indeed disappeared. It would be a real challenge to trace her!

·6·

A Surprising Find

"Mind you, I do not approve of this girl-detective business," Mr Kreutz said. But a slight smile played around his mouth. "Find Manda and maybe I change the mind over. Tell me what you do when you work."

Nancy and her friends were relieved and happy about the change in Mr Kreutz's manner!

"If you feel well enough to go outside, I'll be glad to give you a lesson," said Nancy.

Manda's father got up from the chair. He said that some exercise would help to ease the stiffness in his strained muscles. Nancy started to go to her car for a flashlight.

"No need to do that," said Mr Kreutz. "I'll get a lantern." From underneath the closed-in sink he brought out a paraffin lantern, lighted it, and he and the girls went outside.

"Mama, you come too," said the farmer. "You should learn how the detectives make."

Bess and George were a little puzzled as to what Nancy was going to show Mr Kreutz, until she announced her plan of action. Mr Kreutz was to take the girls on a tour of the barn and other buildings. During the trip they would look for clues which might reveal where Manda possibly had gone.

First, he showed them the spotless dairy, and the girls were amazed to see that many of the stalls were empty. Mrs Kreutz explained that Papa had given most of his cows to their sons.

"We do not need so much milk, butter, and cheese now," she said a little wistfully.

40

Nancy took the light and covered every inch of the floor, searching for a clue. Manda had dropped nothing there. Next, they went into the hay barn. As before, Nancy walked back and forth with the lantern, looking at every inch of the main floor. There was nothing on the immaculately clean boards.

"How do you manage to keep the barn so tidy?" Bess asked Mrs Kreutz.

The woman smiled. "We are House Amish and we hold our religious services in the barn when there are too many people for the house." Mrs Kreutz chuckled. "People say that our barns are cleaner than our homes!"

"I'd like to climb to the loft," said Nancy. "Once when I was a little girl and got hurt on a farm we were visiting I went to the hayloft to have a good cry all by myself. Maybe Manda did the same thing."

"Go ahead," said Mr Kreutz. "There's the ladder."

Nancy scrambled up the rungs and disappeared in the hay. A moment later she called out excitedly, "I've found something!"

Climbing down quickly, she held up a piece of paper. To the complete astonishment of Bess and George they saw the printed words: WITCH TREE.

"Do you know anything about this?" Nancy asked Mr and Mrs Kreutz, watching their expressions intently as they read the strange words.

The couple shook their heads, and the farmer asked Nancy if she thought the paper had been dropped by Manda.

"Possibly," Nancy replied, "but it might have been dropped here by the furniture thief."

"What do you mean?" Mr Kreutz wanted to know.

Nancy reminded him of the hex sign with the strange wording under it which she had found at the Follett mansion. "That's what really brought me up here," she said. "And you do not know what 'witch tree' may mean?"

The Kreutzes insisted that they had no idea what it could possibly mean and were sure that Manda had not, either. "Unless," said Mrs Kreutz, "our daughter learned about it while she was working in Lancaster."

Mr Kreutz shrugged. It was all a mystery to him.

The group inspected the rest of the buildings but found nothing which might give a clue to Manda's whereabouts. The searchers returned to the house, sleepy and ready to retire.

The girls were given two rooms which were as plain as those on the ground floor of the house. Each contained a rope double bed, two small wooden chairs, a small chest, and a curtained-off partition where clothes might be hung.

But one thing was very noticeable in the candlelight. Each piece of furniture was gaily painted with a design of doves and flowers. The beds were covered with patchwork quilts made of pieces of vivid red, green, purple, yellow, and black material.

"I just love it!" exclaimed Bess.

Nancy slept alone and did not waken from the moment she got into bed until a crowing cock roused her the next morning. Her mind refreshed, Nancy began to think at once about the two puzzling mysteries which she hoped to solve. The piece of paper she had found in the Kreutz hayloft with the words "witch tree" on it puzzled her. What was the answer? Manda? Hoelt? Had the two met?

The first thing Nancy did upon entering the kitchen was to ask Mr and Mrs Kreutz if they had ever heard of a Roger Hoelt. At once the farmer said he had known one several years before.

"The fellow lived in Lancaster. When he was just a kid, I caught him in my barn stealing tools. Do you suppose this is the same man?"

Nancy said it no doubt was, because she had learned from the police that Roger Hoelt had once lived in Lancaster and also that he had been imprisoned in New York as a thief.

"I strongly suspect that he's the one who stole the valuable antique furniture in our town and accidentally dropped the paper with the symbol on it. I believe he came back there looking for the paper, but I found it first. Hoelt knows I'm searching for him and has tried to scare me off the case."

Bess declared that probably it was Hoelt and not Manda who had left the "witch tree" paper in the hayloft. "He's still trying to hex you, Nancy," she said worriedly.

Mr Kreutz looked at the girl disapprovingly. "We Amish do not believe in hexing," he said. "There are some non-Amish people in the back country who practise witchcraft."

"They do not all live in the back country, Papa," his wife spoke up quickly. "I was talking to Mrs Dyster at market. She told me about some people in town who think there are certain persons, especially women and girls, who practise witchcraft in secret. If these people hear that someone is a witch, they may be frightened into doing her bodily harm."

Nancy smiled. "Don't worry. My friends and I don't believe in such things," she said, looking straight at Bess. "Roger Hoelt can try hexing me all he pleases. It won't keep me from trying to locate him and the stolen furniture!"

After breakfast the three girls helped Mrs Kreutz clean up the kitchen, then said they must be going. Nancy told the woman that she would combine trying to find Manda with her search for the furniture thief.

The girls went upstairs, straightened their rooms, and packed their suitcases. When they appeared in the kitchen, ready to leave, Mrs Kreutz was amazed.

"You are taking everything with you?" she asked. "Could you not stay by us while you are solving your mystery?"

"Oh, we don't want to wear out our welcome," said Nancy, smiling.

Mrs Kreutz put her hands on her hips. "Such an idea!" she said. Then she smiled. "If you come back here each evening for supper, I can hear how you make about my daughter."

"Well, under those conditions we'll accept your invitation," said Nancy.

Bess giggled: "But if I eat as much supper every night as I did last evening, my family won't recognize me when I return home," she said.

Mrs Kreutz promised to serve a light supper that day. Then she proceeded to name a new menu containing twelve different kinds of food. The girls laughingly commented that they had better start sleuthing and work up good appetites.

"What's our first stop?" George asked, as they started off in the convertible.

"Lancaster," Nancy answered. "I feel so bad about Manda that I'd like to try finding her before we do anything else."

"Me, too," said Bess, and George nodded.

In the city the girls consulted a telephone directory and made a list of all the bakeries in town. Then they went from one to another, asking if Manda Kreutz were there or had ever worked at the shop. All replies were negative until they reached the Stumm Bakery. There the owner said that Manda had worked at the place until a couple of days ago.

"We're very eager to find her," said Nancy. "Have you any idea where she might be?"

"No, I haven't," the woman replied, "unless she went to work for those people that were in here."

"Who are they?" Nancy asked quickly.

"I think they're out-of-town Amish," Mrs Stumm answered. "At least, I had never seen them before. From what I heard of the conversation I gathered that they were just moving here and looking for an Amish girl to help with housework."

Nancy asked the bakery assistant if she had ever heard Manda mention a witch tree. The woman shook her head. Nancy thanked her for the information she had given, bought a bag of *fasnachts*, and joined her friends.

Curious, Bess asked, "What did you buy?" and at the

same time George said, "Did you find out anything about Manda?"

Nancy grinned, opened the bag, and said, "Bess, if you can eat again after that huge breakfast you had, help yourself to a doughnut." To George she replied, "I picked up a possible clue to where Manda went. She may be working for an Amish couple who have just moved into this area."

"That should make it easy," said George.

Referring once more to a classified telephone book, Nancy copied the names of estate agents in town. This time, the girls divided the work of calling on them and half an hour later met at the car. None of them had found a single clue to the wanted couple.

"There's just one chance," said Nancy. "One of the men told me that old farms sometimes change hands in a direct sale. We'll keep asking. Now let's go to Mr Zinn's."

For a change George drove, and Nancy gave directions to Alpha Zinn's home. Fortunately, they found it without any trouble. The place looked a great deal like the Kreutz farm, only the buildings were smaller.

"I suggest," said Nancy, "that we just pretend to be buying antiques."

"Okay," replied George. "If we find out he has the furniture from River Heights, that mystery will be solved promptly."

"And if we don't," added Nancy, "which I don't think we will, then our case is just beginning."

Alpha Zinn's appearance bore out his cousin's remark about his great love of eating. But the roly-poly, smiling relative of Mrs Tenney did not look like a man who was not to be trusted. Nevertheless, Nancy was on her guard.

"I see you have an out-of-state licence," the man remarked as the girls walked into a small building marked *Office*. "You are interested in antiques?"

Nancy replied that they would like to see what he had.

When Mr Zinn asked if they wanted to see anything in particular, Nancy told him that they would like to look round.

The dealer led the way to a large barn, where the girls stared in amazement at the quantity of furniture on display. Not only was the main floor filled, but two haylofts had been completely cleaned out and were stacked with furniture.

Nancy whispered to George and Bess to hold the man's attention while she made a tour by herself. In her handbag she had a list and description of pieces taken from the Follett homestead. Mrs Tenney had given it to her just before Nancy left River Heights, together with a sketch of the George Washington tables.

Nancy's plan worked admirably. Soon she found herself a good distance from the other three. Taking Mrs Tenney's list from her handbag, she began a systematic hunt for the stolen antiques. Most of the furniture on the list was of dark wood, while Mr Zinn's pieces were of pine or maple.

In a corner, however, Nancy saw a small cherry table. Instantly her heart began to beat a little faster. Looking at the sketch in her hand she compared it with the table. It matched perfectly!

·7·

An Accident

Suddenly Mr Zinn noticed that Nancy was not with the group. "Where is your friend?" he asked.

Flustered, Bess stammered, "Oh, I guess she's just looking round."

The antique dealer eyed the girls suspiciously. "Is she, by any chance, snooping for some reason?"

George rushed to Nancy's defence. "My friend is a nice girl!" she said haughtily.

"Well, you never can tell about people," said Mr Zinn. "I've lost some valuable articles from my shop. Mind you, I'm not saying your friend would take anything, but I have to be careful. You understand?"

The girls had prolonged the conversation as much as they dared. Hoping that Nancy had had enough time to look round, they started back through the vast barn. At the same moment they saw her hurrying towards them.

"Did you find something you liked?" the dealer asked, looking at her intently.

"There is one piece which interests me very much," the young detective replied. "It's that small, unusual cherry table in the corner."

She led the way back and pointed out the table about which she was suspicious.

"Oh, that. If you like it, buy it. The table's not so expensive," Mr Zinn answered. "It's a copy I made of a George Washington antique—a very good copy if I do say so myself. I am a cabinetmaker as well as antique dealer."

The man's statement that the table was a copy came as a

great surprise to Nancy and her friends, George and Bess.

"Where is the original piece?" George asked.

"Well, actually there are two of them," the dealer replied. "One is in River Heights. I have no idea where the matching table is, but I've searched antique shops and made many inquiries. I'd certainly like to get my hands on that piece!"

The girls glanced at one another. Evidently Mr Zinn was not aware that Mrs Follett had owned the matching table!

His eyes gleaming, the man went on, "The original tables have hidden drawers in them. It's said that one of them holds a great secret."

This announcement startled the three girls. Did Mrs Tenney know this? Could it be one of the reasons she suspected her cousin of taking the antique furniture?

"That certainly is an unusual story," Bess remarked. "Please tell us more about it, Mr Zinn."

The antique dealer replied that there was really nothing more to tell. He had had a great-aunt, named Mrs Sara Follett, who had recently passed away. She had left the contents of her home to be divided between Mr Zinn and his cousin, Mrs Tenney, who lived in River Heights.

"As soon as the estate is settled, my cousin and I will have to decide how to apportion the furniture. It will be difficult, because we've never been very friendly. One thing we'll both probably want is the George Washington table. It's by far the most valuable piece of the collection."

"Is the secret in Mrs Follett's table?" Bess questioned him.

"No, it's not. I purchased the table for my aunt from another dealer," Mr Zinn said. "While it was here in my shop being refinished, an old friend of mine from Lancaster happened to come in. He recognized the table from a picture he had once seen and asked me if I had looked in the secret drawer. Up to that point I had not known there was one. It was very cleverly constructed."

Mr Zinn and his friend had gone over the table thoroughly

and finally had found the hidden drawer. But to their disappointment there was nothing in it.

"So whatever it is must be in the matching table," Mr Zinn went on. "That's why I'd like to find it."

Nancy decided that it was only fair to the man to tell him what she already knew. Unless he were a clever actor, he was not aware of the furniture theft.

Without divulging the fact that Mrs Tenney had asked her to investigate him, Nancy told Mr Zinn that the three girls were from River Heights and that his cousin was a neighbour of hers.

"A few days ago she asked me to accompany her to your great-aunt's mansion," Nancy went on. "When we got there, we found that a burglar had been at work." As Nancy said this, she closely watched the man.

"What!" Mr Zinn shouted. His face turned red and his neck muscles grew taut. "The furniture was stolen?"

As Nancy nodded she came to the conclusion that Mr Zinn had had no part in the disappearance of the Follett collection. He could not possibly have responded in this way to her unexpected disclosure if he were guilty.

"There were two Washington tables in the collection," she said.

"Only one was genuine," Mr Zinn informed her. "I made the other for Aunt Sara."

. Nancy was glad to have this straightened out. She now decided to tell him about the hex sign that she had found and went on with her story. When she finished, she showed him the paper that she had found in the Follett mansion and asked if he had ever seen the symbol.

"I can't say that I have," the dealer replied. "But on the other hand, it does look familiar. That may be because it is similar to many I have seen."

Nancy inquired if he knew a Roger Hoelt or had ever heard of him.

"Well, now, let me think," Mr Zinn answered. "Oh, yes,

now I remember. There was a fellow named Hoelt in my class in high school. I don't think his first name was Roger, though."

"But it proves," said Nancy, "that people named Hoelt do live around this area." And Mr Zinn nodded.

The antique dealer was anxious to know what was being done to apprehend the thief and find the stolen furniture. "This is a crime—a crime!" he said.

Nancy told him that the River Heights police were working on the case. Then she added, "I wonder if the thief knows the story of the secret drawer in the Washington table. If he does, that would account for his stealing the tables Mrs Follett had. He didn't know only one was genuine."

"That's right," Mr Zinn agreed. "Maybe the thief has already looked in another matching table. When he didn't find the secret, he decided maybe the table was a copy. Then, later, he thought the two Mrs Follett had must be genuine."

Bess sighed. "This is too much for me," she said. "Let's go, Nancy. It's almost lunchtime and I'm starved."

Nancy laughed but George looked at her cousin disapprovingly. "Miss Marvin," she said in a severe tone, "you had a big breakfast and three doughnuts since. You ought not to eat until tomorrow!"

"It must be the country air," Bess defended herself.

At this moment a woman appeared in the barn shop. Mr Zinn introduced her as his wife. She was as round as her husband and looked even plumper in her full skirt, shirred light-blue apron, and ruffled collar and sleeves. But her face was dimpled and pretty, and she had a radiant smile.

"Mama," said the antique dealer, "these girls are from River Heights. Nancy is a friend of my cousin Ruth Tenney. Mama, she brings us dreadful news. Aunt Sara's most valuable antiques have been stolen!"

Mrs Zinn's smile faded. "Stolen!" she cried. "That is wicked!"

After Nancy quickly retold the story, Mrs Zinn said sadly, "Papa, that is a great loss to you, ain't?"

Her husband tried to hide his distress. "What one does not own is never a loss," he told her. "It is a great disappointment, of course, but perhaps the furniture will be found."

After a few more minutes of conversation about the loss, Mrs Zinn said, "Papa, I came to tell you that dinner is ready. Lock up and come to table." Turning to the visitors, she added, "It would please us to have you break bread with us."

"Oh, that would be wonderful!" exclaimed Bess at once, not giving Nancy and George a chance to refuse.

Mrs Zinn was pleased that her invitation had been accepted and led the girls to the farmhouse. Inside, it was far different from that of the Kreutzes. It was gay with flowers, window curtains, and quaint hand-made rugs. On the table, set in the dining room, was a cloth hand-embroidered in blue and red pigeons.

Quickly Mrs Zinn set three more places and soon the five were eating a meal almost as sumptuous as that served at the Kreutzes'. Dessert was shoofly pie and at once Bess asked how it was made.

"Molasses, sugar, eggs, and spices," Mrs Zinn replied, but did not offer to give the amount of the ingredients. The girls could see that she highly prized the recipe and wanted to keep it a secret.

The Zinns asked where the girls were staying. When they replied at the Kreutz farm, Mr Zinn frowned. "That man is too strict," he said. "He never allowed his daughter Manda to have a good time. He never wanted her to go out to meet young men. He said he would pick her a husband. That's why she ran away. You know she ran away?"

The girls said yes, but that Mr and Mrs Kreutz now wanted Nancy to find their daughter and persuade her to come home.

"We picked up a clue this morning that she might be

working for an Amish couple who moved into this area recently," Nancy said. "Have you any idea who they might be?"

"No, I haven't," said Mr Zinn, "but if I get any leads, I'll let you know."

An hour later the girls left the farm and started back for the Kreutz place. When they were about three miles from their destination, Bess, looking out the back window, said nervously that she thought they were being followed by a car.

"Maybe the hex on you is working again," she told Nancy.

With a look of disgust, George told her cousin to stop talking nonsense. At this moment there came the loud blast of a horn. Nancy pulled over to the side of the road. The car which Bess had worried about shot past them at high speed. The girls caught only a fleeting glimpse of the Amish driver. He had a beard and his black hat was pulled far down over his ears.

"That man's a speed demon," Bess cried indignantly.

"Oh," George remarked, "he's probably late for some appointment." She grinned at Bess. "Anyway, he didn't follow us for long."

The car sped ahead in a cloud of dust and was soon out of sight. A short while later, Nancy, keeping within the speed limit, came to a sharp curve round a low hillside.

As she turned the corner, Nancy gasped in dismay. Strewn across the road, directly in the path of the car, were large concrete bricks. There was no chance to avoid ploughing into them.

Quickly Nancy put her foot on the brake, but not soon enough to avoid hitting several of the bricks full force. All three girls were thrown violently forward. Bess, seated in the middle, struck her head on the mirror and blacked out!

·8·

Witches

When Bess blacked out, she fell against George. Quickly George and Nancy opened the car door, got out, and laid the unconscious girl on the seat.

"Bess!" Nancy exclaimed.

As she and George leaned over her, worried, Bess's eyelids raised and she looked up at them. At once she tried to sit up but the other girls told her to take it easy. "Are you all right?" George asked.

"Yes," said Bess. She felt her forehead. "Ow!" she moaned. "I really gave my head a bang."

"All of us might have been killed," cried George indignantly. "Whoever could have been so careless?"

Nancy declared, after noting a nearby building site where a house and a pile of bricks were at the side of the road, that it seemed like more than carelessness. It looked as if the concrete bricks had been deliberately tossed on to the road.

"The hex is working," Bess muttered.

Her cousin gave her a dark look, then she and Nancy started to carry the bricks out of the way, so that they could drive on.

Bess, not feeling up to helping them, got out of the car and idly watched. The others were almost finished with their task when a piece of paper, stuck into an opening of one of the bricks, caught her eye.

Bess walked over to it, picked up the paper, and discovered handwriting on it.

"Listen to this! Here's a note. It says: '*Nancy Drew, witches are not wanted in Amish country*.' "

Nancy and George rushed to Bess's side and read the note themselves.

"This explains a lot," said Nancy. "That man who rushed past us was Roger Hoelt in disguise! He knew these bricks were here and threw them in the road and left this note!"

The cousins gasped. "You're right," said George, "and we're going after him. Come on!"

The girls quickly got into the car and started off. Bess remarked that the man had such a head start they would never be able to find him.

"We'll watch for his tyre tracks in the dust," said Nancy.

The young sleuth pointed out that this was not a well-travelled road. Moreover, it was an extremely dusty one. It should be easy to trail the man.

As they hurried along, Nancy said she had a whole new slant on the case. The couple for whom Manda might be working were Roger Hoelt and his wife.

"You mean they're posing as an Amish couple?" George asked.

"Yes. Since he once lived here, he'd know just how to do it. I doubt that he'll suspect we've guessed it, though, and will take bigger chances than he might otherwise."

"But he'll be dangerous just the same," Bess warned. "By the way, how long are we going to follow Roger Hoelt or whoever it was that left the note?"

"To the highway," Nancy answered. "This road doesn't cross it according to the map, so the man we're pursuing would have had to turn on to the highway. After that, it will be pretty hopeless to follow his tracks."

Reaching the main road, Nancy turned left as the man in the car ahead of her apparently had done, judging by the tyre marks in the dusty road. She sped along for nearly a mile but did not overtake him.

Finally Bess pleaded that they give up the chase. "I have a dreadful headache," she said. "Please, let's go back to the Kreutzes'."

"Of course," said Nancy kindly. "Why didn't you tell me before?"

She turned round and drove back to the Kreutz farm. Manda's mother came out to greet them. "Did you find any trace of my daughter?" she asked quickly.

As Nancy alighted, she told the woman about the Amish couple for whom Manda might be working. "Tomorrow we'll make a further search to locate them," she promised.

Mrs Kreutz looked at Bess, who was being helped out of the car by George. "Why, look at your head!" she cried solicitously. "What happened?"

"We had to stop suddenly and I bumped it," Bess replied.

From their years of friendship with the young detective, Bess and George had learned to let Nancy act as spokesman. She seemed to know just how much to reveal, whereas they were afraid they might give information that Nancy would prefer to keep secret for the time being.

Nancy told Mrs Kreutz about the concrete bricks being thrown in the road, and her inability to stop the car in time to avoid running into them. But she said nothing about the note or her suspicions regarding the Hoelts.

They all went into the house and George asked, "Have you something we can put on Bess's head? It's aching badly."

"Yes, I have some home-made liniment," Mrs Kreutz replied. "But I will do a little powwowing too. Come upstairs."

After bringing the bottle of liniment and a cloth to Bess's bedroom, she told the girl to lie down. Sprinkling the folded cloth with the liniment, the woman laid it on Bess's forehead. Then she went for her *Ga-brauch Buch*. After turning several pages, she came to the one she wanted and let the book lie open on her lap.

In a low voice she began to read from it in German. The three girls could understand little of it. Mrs Kreutz now gently stroked Bess's head, then her arms.

Finally the woman closed her eyes and began to mumble to herself. Nancy and George wondered if she were repeating words from the *Ga-brauch Buch* or whether she was praying. A few minutes later Bess heaved a sigh, then closed her eyes and fell asleep.

Mrs Kreutz seemed to be unaware of anything but her powwow. But presently she stopped speaking, arose, and motioned to Nancy and George to follow her from the bedroom. They closed the door and all went downstairs.

Abruptly Mrs Kreutz's mood changed completely. Smiling, she asked the two girls if they would like to help her prepare dinner. "We will have moon pies tonight," she said.

"And I'll bet they'll taste out of this world," George said with a laugh.

"That is a good joke," Mrs Kreutz said. "And I suppose you have never heard of them. Come. We will prepare a dozen."

She took some piecrust dough, already mixed, rolled it out on a table and floured it. Then she told the girls to cut the dough into round sections six inches in diameter. This done, she asked George to go outside to the small stone house through which a stream of cold water flowed. Here crocks of milk, cream, cheeses, and meats were kept cool.

"Bring the roast of veal," the woman directed. "It stands behind on the top shelf over."

George grinned, wondering if she would ever find the veal! But presently she came back to the kitchen with it.

Mrs Kreutz cut off a generous piece of the meat, put it into a wooden chopping bowl, and cut it up finely with an old-fashioned chopper. The meat was now transferred to a skillet on the stove. Butter, cream, salt, pepper, and pickled relish were added. After it had cooked a while, Mrs Kreutz directed the girls to butter each of the piecrusts. Then into one half of each she put generous spoonfuls of the meat.

"Now pull the lids over one half and pinch the edges all around with your thumb," she instructed.

"Oh, they look just like half-moons," George declared.

Mrs Kreutz said more butter should be spread on the top, then the moon pies would be ready for the oven. "Papa likes these for dinner," she stated. "By the way, do not mention Manda to Papa. When he is ready to talk about her, he will ask you." Nancy and George agreed to wait.

Within an hour Bess came downstairs, saying she felt much better. "Thank you for the treatment," she said to Mrs Kreutz. "And doesn't something smell good! Mm-mm!"

George laughed. "Bess must be back to normal—she's hungry!" Then she told her cousin of Mrs Kreutz's request not to mention Manda.

As promised, the girls said nothing about his daughter when Mr Kreutz walked into the kitchen. He said good evening to the girls and they all sat down to eat. During the meal he did not bring up the subject of his missing daughter. Instead, he talked about his crops. But as soon as the dishes had been washed, he called Nancy aside and asked her what she had learned about Manda. As the others listened, Nancy told him in detail. At the end she said, "Mr Kreutz, I think you should notify the police. They may know who has moved into this area recently and locate Manda easily."

"No!" Mr Kreutz cried in a loud voice, pounding the arm of his chair with his fist. "I am an Amish man. We take care of family matters without the help of the police. No, I gave my permission to you to locate my daughter. But no one else outside the Kreutz family will be allowed to interfere."

Suddenly he rose from his chair and reached for a Bible that lay on the window sill. "I will read a few passages," he said. "Then we will pray for Manda."

The girls listened attentively to the High German he read and bowed their heads when he did. At the end there was a short silence, then the farmer asked Nancy to tell him what else she had done that day.

As she talked, Mr and Mrs Kreutz listened with half-hearted interest, but when Nancy reached the part of her story about the note in the concrete brick, the farmer cried out:

"*Du bin en hex maydel!*"

"But I'm not a witch girl!" Nancy protested, amazed that evidently he now believed the superstition.

Despite her denial, Mr and Mrs Kreutz at once became quite cool towards all the girls. Both of them said it was time to go to bed and nodded a curt goodnight. The girls climbed the stairs, nonplussed by the change in attitude.

As they undressed, the three spoke in whispers. "This settles it," said Bess. "We'll move out in the morning."

"Yes. We're certainly not wanted," George agreed. "Imagine their believing that you're a witch, Nancy!"

Their friend, with a mystified expression, asked herself, "But why are the Kreutzes so convinced all of a sudden that I am a witch? There's something to this they haven't told us!"

·9·

A Stolen Horse

The sudden change in the attitude of the Kreutzes towards the girls bothered them so much that they slept fitfully. Although the farmer had said he did not believe in hexing, yet when Nancy had shown him the note about witches, he had acted as if she were one!

"If people in this area are going to act afraid of me," Nancy thought, "I'll certainly have a difficult time trying to solve the mystery."

Although Nancy had no idea of giving up the case because of such an attitude, Bess was of a different frame of mind. Sensitive by nature, she did not want to stay where she would be shunned. Besides, she felt that further work on the mystery would involve more danger all the time. "I'll try to talk Nancy into leaving this Amish territory," she decided.

As for George, she was angry with the Kreutzes. After Nancy and her friends had done their best to locate a girl who had run away, her parents were now treating their guests as suspects!

Early the following morning, Nancy and the girls packed their bags and went downstairs. Mr and Mrs Kreutz were already at the table having breakfast. They nodded, but did not invite the girls to join them.

"We're leaving," said Nancy. "I'm sorry that you've been disturbed by rumours about me and that you evidently believe them. I strongly suspect that Roger Hoelt is behind all of this. Some day he'll be caught, then I'll be cleared of these silly charges."

59

Nancy's hope that her words might convince Mr and Mrs Kreutz was not fulfilled. The farmer and his wife merely nodded again, and did not get up even to say goodbye. Nevertheless, each of the girls thanked the couple for their hospitality, then walked out the kitchen door. In silence they got into Nancy's convertible and drove off.

"Well, I've never been so badly treated by nice people in all my life!" George stormed.

"Maybe we shouldn't blame them too much," Nancy suggested. "There may be more to this than we realize. But I intend to find out what it is!"

"Will you keep on looking for Manda?" Bess asked Nancy.

"Certainly. If she's working for a thief, I want to warn her as soon as possible."

"Maybe," Bess surmised, "the Kreutzes think you know where Manda is and won't tell them."

"That's possible. They may have been told some witch is responsible for Manda's disappearance and now they believe I'm that person."

"I'd like to bet," said George, "that if we bring Manda back, the Kreutzes will do an about face."

Bess wanted to know what place Nancy was heading for. Nancy said she thought they might try New Holland. It was a good base from which to work.

"I'd like to do some inquiring in that area."

In New Holland they found a place to eat and ordered breakfast.

"We'd better keep this witch business to ourselves," Nancy advised, "or we may not find a place to sleep."

Bess and George smiled, and Nancy asked the woman in charge if she could recommend a boarding-house. The woman suggested a place about a mile out of town.

"Papa Glick had a bad accident two years ago and had to give up farming," the woman said. "Now he is a *schumacher*. Mama Glick will rent rooms sometimes. The Glicks are Church Amish. You will be very comfortable there."

When the girls finished eating they went directly to the farm. It was well kept, although many of the fields were in pasture. The house was of red brick. The barn, of wood, was also red.

A pleasant-faced woman, wearing a green dress and the traditional Amish cap and apron, opened the door. When Nancy stated the reason for the girls' call, Mrs Glick invited them in.

"I have four rooms empty," she said. "Make your choice between."

The interior of the house, with its homespun curtains and floor coverings, was quaint and attractive. The upstairs bedrooms were spanking clean and just as cheerful. The girls were delighted and at once chose the rooms they would take.

"You are sight-seeing in New Holland?" Mrs Glick asked.

"Yes, we are," Nancy replied. Feeling she could confide in this pleasant woman, she added, "And we're also here for another reason." She told about the stolen furniture for which they were looking and their suspicion that the thief might be hiding in Amish territory.

At this moment the girls heard footsteps on the stairs and a boy and girl appeared. Mrs Glick introduced them as Becky, aged ten, her daughter, and Henner, eight, her son.

"They're adorable, and how healthy looking!" Bess exclaimed.

Both children had big brown eyes and very straight bodies. Their hair was cut and combed Amish style.

Becky wore a prayer cap just like her mother's and carried a black bonnet. She had on a long black smock over a white blouse, a white apron but no shawl.

Henner held a small-sized Amish man's hat in his hand. The boy's blue shirt, black trousers, and wide home-made braces were exactly the same as the girls had seen all the Amish men wearing.

"Henner," said his mother, "I'm sorry to see you so dirty when we have visitors. Did you fall?"

His sister answered for him. "Henner, he goes by horse stall down. *Iss er net schuslich?*"

"Yes, he is careless," his mother agreed. "Henner, go scrub yourself."

The girls went downstairs to get their luggage and then unpacked. Half an hour later they were ready to take up their sleuthing. Just as they were leaving, they heard hoof-beats and saw an Amish carriage coming up the lane. The horse's sleek body gleamed and so did the newly varnished black vehicle he was pulling. The carriage was plain, with no dashboard or other trimming. It had a front and rear seat, and was almost completely enclosed.

"*Papa kumpt hame!*" the children cried, and ran to meet him.

Mrs Glick went outside with the girls and introduced her husband, a nice-looking, kindly man, but pale compared to Amish farmers they had seen.

After greeting him, Nancy told Mr Glick what had brought the girls to Pennsylvania Dutch country. The cobbler had not heard of Roger Hoelt, he said, and was sorry to learn about the stolen furniture.

Nancy asked, "Mr and Mrs Glick, do you know Manda Kreutz?"

The couple exchanged glances, then Papa Glick said, "Yes," and added, "We do not approve of young girls running away from home. But maybe her father was too strict. Now she has taken up with Amish strangers."

"Please tell me about it," Nancy begged. "Where is Manda?"

"I do not know," Mr Glick replied. "But she was seen riding in a carriage with a couple who told a friend of mine, Mr Weiss, they are from Ohio."

"Is he sure they are Amish?" Nancy asked.

"My friend wonders," the cobbler answered, "because of their speech. He thinks they might be English."

When Nancy inquired what Mr Glick meant by the last remark, he explained that among his sect, any non-Amish people are called English, meaning foreigners.

"This pair wore Amish costumes," he said, "and had an Amish carriage, but maybe they were just putting on."

Nancy was excited over this latest piece of information. Her hunch had probably been right. The couple were Mr and Mrs Roger Hoelt! If Manda Kreutz became too friendly with them, she might get into serious trouble with the law!

"We're trying to find Manda," Nancy told the Glicks. "Her parents want her to come home. Can you give us any other clues?" she asked the cobbler. He regretfully shook his head.

Nancy had a sudden inspiration. "If the Hoelts are masquerading," she said aloud, "they probably bought a horse and carriage around here recently."

"Unless they stole them," George interposed.

"That could easily be done," Mrs Glick spoke up. "Amish carriages all look alike. It is pretty difficult to distinguish one from another."

Then she smiled a little. "The owners have funny ways of telling them apart—a bullet hole from rifle practice or a high board on the floor for a short-legged wife."

Mr Glick insisted that an owner did not even need earmarks to tell his carriage from others. "We chust look at 'em. We know 'em!" he said.

Nancy told Mr Glick that she suspected the man masquerading as Amish might be the furniture thief and she would like to inquire at local carriage factories about any recent purchase by an out-of-state man. The cobbler gave her the name of a factory five miles away and the girls set off at once for the place. At the carriage factory Nancy spoke to the manager and stated the reason for her call.

"You have come to the right place to find out," the man said. "But the carriage was not purchased. It was stolen!"

"Stolen!" Nancy gasped, glancing at Bess and George.

"Do you know who took the carriage?" the manager asked.

"No. By the way, have you ever met a Roger Hoelt?"

"Never heard of him."

Nancy remarked that maybe the thief had also stolen a horse to go with the carriage.

"You have the nail on the head hit," the man said. "My uncle, who lives a few miles from here, has a lot of horses. He missed one the same day my carriage was stolen."

"What colour was the horse?" Nancy asked him.

"Black."

Nancy thanked the manager, then the girls hurried outside to discuss what they had learned.

"So now," said George, "we start roaming the countryside looking for a fake Amish man driving a black horse and carriage." She chuckled. "Who wants the honour of pulling off his false beard?"

·10·

A Harsh Accusation

"There's one thing I'm glad of," declared Bess as the girls drove back towards New Holland. "We don't have to return to the Kreutzes' and tell them that their daughter has taken up with a thief."

"If Manda really is with the Hoelts," said Nancy quickly, "I'm sure that she's entirely unaware of what they're doing."

George pointed out that, nevertheless, the Amish girl might have to testify in a court case if the Hoelts were apprehended. "That would just about crush her proud mother and father," she said.

Presently Nancy noticed that they were not far from the road which led to the Zinn house. She suggested that they stop there and tell Mr Zinn what they had learned regarding the Hoelts. It was also possible that he might have additional news for them.

"Besides," said Nancy, "he has no idea where we're staying now in case he should want to get in touch with us."

Turning the car into a side road, Nancy drove directly to the antique dealer's farm. In his office the girls found the man wearing a broad smile. He greeted them happily, announcing jubilantly that business had been brisk and profitable.

"I've sold many pieces of furniture since yesterday morning," he said. "And at good prices, too. Well, have you any news for me of the stolen antiques?"

Before Nancy could reply, Mr Zinn went on, "You remember that cherry table—the copy of the George Washington piece—you were interested in?"

As the girls nodded, he continued, "That was one of the articles I sold." He chuckled. "A couple came in here who were interested in buying it. I named a high price, expecting them to bargain me down. But they never said a word about the price and bought the table."

Again Nancy started to tell what she had heard about Mr and Mrs Hoelt possibly being in the neighbourhood, but Mr Zinn gave her no opportunity.

He rambled on, "Funny thing about that couple. They're Amish, but they don't live round here. Came from Ohio. It's a long distance for them to drive in a carriage," he mused.

Nancy, Bess, and George were astonished.

"Was this man driving a black horse?" Nancy queried.

"Yes," Mr Zinn replied. "What made you ask that?"

This time, he waited for Nancy to answer, and she told him of her suspicion that Hoelt was masquerading.

"It's very likely he has found out the George Washington tables he stole don't contain the secret he's looking for," Nancy deduced.

Mr Zinn chuckled. "And because of the high price I set on my copy of the table," he said, "he figured it must be the genuine matching piece."

"Exactly!"

Suddenly Mr Zinn's expression changed from one of elation to concern. "You mean I had the thief who stole my inheritance right in my shop and let him get away?" the antique dealer shouted, his face growing red with anger.

"I'm afraid so," said Nancy. Then, on a sudden hunch, she asked, "How did this man pay for the table?"

"In cash," Mr Zinn replied.

"May I see the money?" the young detective requested.

The man unlocked his old-fashioned, roll-top desk and took out a tin box. From this he removed a roll of twenty-dollar notes. "Here's what the fellow gave me," he said.

Nancy took a similar note from her wallet and compared

it with the other twenties. First, she compared the letter, plate, and serial numbers, and the series identification with Mr Zinn's money. All seemed to be in order.

Next, she compared the paper quality, knowing that genuine United States currency has a distinctive feel. They were identical as far as she could tell.

While the group watched breathlessly, Nancy examined the design on the border of the face and back plates of each note. Now she frowned—in this respect they were lacking in continuity and uniformity of shading.

"Look!" she exclaimed, and pointed out the variance there was in the twenty-dollar bills from her own, which was sharp and clear.

Suddenly Mr Zinn cried out, "Those bills the man gave me—is counterfeit *gelt*!"

"Yes. I'm pretty sure they are," Nancy agreed.

The man was very upset. He paced back and forth in his office. Finally Nancy asked him if he were not going to call the police and tell them about the counterfeit money.

"*Ya! Ya!*" the dealer said. He fumbled through the telephone book looking for the number of the police station. Finally he handed Nancy the book and asked her to do it.

"All that money!" he mumbled to himself. "Even if I did overcharge him, that table was worth quite a lot!"

Nancy found the number and made the call. Then she handed the receiver to Mr Zinn. The local police captain said that he would send a counterfeit expert down at once to examine the money.

In a short time two officers arrived. One immediately said the bills were fake. The other policeman wrote down a description of the couple who had bought the table.

"We'll send out a message to the state police," one of the officers said. "We ought to pick up the two of them in no time."

The girls stayed to wait for a report. But as the hours passed there was no news that the couple had been caught.

Mrs Zinn, more philosophical than her husband about the loss, did not let it bother her. At midday she served the girls a tremendous meal. A short while after they finished eating, George caught Bess secretly weighing herself on a set of scales in the barn.

Peering over her cousin's shoulder, she exclaimed, "Bess Marvin! You've gained five pounds since you left home!"

Bess was embarrassed momentarily but insisted that George also get on the scale. The girl with the tomboyish figure was aghast at the weight that she too had put on.

"If this keeps up," she said, chuckling, "I'll have to go out in the fields and walk behind a horse-drawn plough for two solid hours to lose the extra pounds!"

Late in the afternoon, the girls were upstairs in the Zinn house. They were looking at several patchwork quilts which Mrs Zinn had made with the help of her neighbours, when her husband rushed into the house.

"Where's Nancy Drew?" he shouted, and from the tone of his voice the girls knew that he was angry.

"We must go down at once," Mrs Zinn said. "Papa is upset."

She and the visitors hurried to the kitchen, where Mr Zinn stood with his feet far apart and his hands on his hips. He glared at Nancy. "So this is how you work!" he cried. "You come round here pretending to be friends and this is what you do to me!"

Nancy was nonplussed. She hardly knew what to reply. But she finally asked him what he meant.

"As if you did not know," he said, shaking a finger at her. "But I have friends and you've been found out! You thought you could get away with those two valuable lamps of mine, but you didn't do it!"

The young detective stared in utter bewilderment. Had the man gone out of his mind? George, who had been growing angrier by the moment during the man's recital, demanded that he explain his accusations.

"Those two lamps in your car!" Mr Zinn roared. "How long have they been there? Did you take them yesterday or today? The woman told me you're a witch and now I believe it!"

"Oh, Papa, do not say such things!" his wife pleaded.

It was several minutes before she could calm the man enough for him to give an explanation. A young woman had telephoned to warn him that a girl by the name of Nancy Drew from River Heights who looked very innocent was really a witch and a thief. She was driving round the countryside stealing small valuable antiques.

"The woman told me," said Zinn, "that if I looked in her car I would no doubt find something from my shop. Well, I did. Nancy Drew, I'm going to call the police!"

Disturbing Rumours

Mrs Zinn rushed to her husband's side and grabbed his hands. "Papa, your asthma will return if you get so mad," she said. "These girls cannot be thieves. They are nice people. They are trying to help you."

The irate antique dealer looked impatiently at his wife, then glared at Nancy. "I found my stolen lamps hidden under a blanket on the back seat of your car. How can you explain that?"

Nancy tried not to raise her voice, although she too was becoming angry. "Did the woman who called you give her name?" she asked.

Mr Zinn admitted that she had not, but the woman had told such a convincing story of seeing Nancy secreting the lamps that he had believed her. Finding the evidence in the convertible had convinced him that Nancy was guilty.

Nancy was stunned by the accusation. "I'm sure this is Roger Hoelt's work," she declared. "He got his wife to make the call. He has been trying in various ways to keep me from working on the case. It started while I was still in River Heights."

"Yes," George broke in. "If this whole idea about Nancy stealing lamps was not utterly foolish, I'd call our chief of police in River Heights and have him tell you a few things!"

Bess added indignantly, "If you only knew all the wonderful things Nancy has done in her life, you wouldn't dare say these things about her."

With his wife and the three girls against him, Mr Zinn

calmed down a little. Finally he said he would not call the police because he now had the lamps. But he said firmly that he wanted the girls to leave the premises immediately.

"That suits me," said George. "If we had taken your old lamps, don't you think we'd have left long before this?"

Mrs Zinn looked as though she wanted to cry. She had become fond of the girls and did not want them to leave her house with ill feelings towards her husband. Once more the kindly woman tried to reason with him, but the man was adamant.

"We can solve our own mysteries," he told her. "There may be something to this witch business, after all. There are all types of witches!"

Nancy's eyes flashed. This insult was too much! She said goodbye to Mrs Zinn, turned on her heel, and walked away. Bess and George followed.

The girls drove off without a backward look. Their feelings were mixed. Roger Hoelt and his wife had played a clever trick this time in accusing Nancy of being a thief. Besides, she was becoming more unpopular by the moment in the Amish neighbourhood. Soon no one would be willing to speak to the young detective or trust her.

"Well, at least you didn't go to jail," said George. Then, trying to bring a little humour into the situation, she said, "We all look like witches sometimes, especially after we've washed our hair! Particularly me!"

Nancy suddenly grinned and said, "I have an old witch Halloween costume at home. Maybe I should have brought it along!"

But Bess could see no humour in their predicament. She was afraid that if Mr Zinn spread the lamp story—and she would not put it past him to do so—the girls might even be asked to leave the county. "By the time we return to the Glicks', they may turn against us too, and throw us out," she prophesied dolefully.

It was with some apprehension that the girls drove up the

lane leading to the Glick farmhouse. Becky and Henner
rushed out of the kitchen door to meet them. Before the girls
could even step from the convertible, Henner called out:

"You be witches, ain't?"

Nancy stepped to the ground and, kneeling, put her arms
around the little boy. Quietly but firmly she told him that she
and her friends were not witches. "Pinch me and see," she
suggested. "I'm just as real as you are."

"But Mama, she went to a *schnitzing*," Henner told her.
"The women—they say you all be witches."

At this moment Mrs Glick ran from the house. Having
overheard her son's remark, she scolded him, saying, "I told
you, Henner, that witches are only make-believe. You are a
bad boy for repeating what I told your papa those silly
women said. Go help him now."

Mrs Glick turned to the three girls, as her children ran off.
"My friends are not really foolish," she said. "But some of
them are superstitious. They believe strange stories. They
forget that witches are nothing but old wives' tales!" She
smiled in a friendly way and the girls felt relieved.

They all went into the house and Nancy excused herself to
freshen up for supper. While washing her hands and face,
she reviewed her problem. The girl detective was sure that
Roger Hoelt and his wife were spreading the propaganda
which was making her unpopular with the Amish people.
But how to cope with it was a big question.

Just then, she heard a car coming up the farmhouse lane.
Peering from her bedroom window, Nancy saw that it had
stopped at the kitchen entrance. A uniformed state policeman got out and knocked loudly on the door.

A few moments later Mrs Glick called up the stairway,
"Nancy, will you come downstairs, please?"

Nancy fairly flew to the ground floor, hoping that the
policeman had some news of Roger Hoelt and his wife.
Perhaps they had been apprehended! Mrs Glick introduced
her to the officer, a freckle-faced, outdoor-type man.

"How do you do?" the officer acknowledged the introduction. "Well, you certainly don't look much like a witch."

Nancy was thunderstruck! Did the police in this area believe the foolish rumours, too, or was he joking?

Before she could reply, however, the policeman grinned. He explained that earlier in the day a call had been received at police headquarters. An unidentified woman had said that three out-of-state girls were stirring up trouble among neighbourhood families. The girls, she had said, were witches. And one in particular, named Nancy Drew, had claimed she had supernatural powers to locate missing persons and solve mysteries.

"Well, I never—" said Mrs Glick.

The policeman smiled. "It's all nonsense, of course. But our practice is to investigate anonymous calls whenever possible. I traced you here to the Glicks'. How about it, Miss Drew, can you clear this up?"

Nancy told the officer everything that had happened so far, and for the first time Mrs Glick heard the story of the hex sign with the words "witch tree symbol" under it. The woman blinked in amazement.

Continuing, the girl detective admitted to having solved several mysteries but said that she was only an amateur and laid no claim to being an expert. She added that she had in no way tried to create trouble in the neighbourhood.

At this moment, George, who had been listening on the stairway, came down and corroborated Nancy's story. Then she asked about Roger Hoelt and was told that he had not been apprehended.

The officer said that the police would do their best to stop the witch rumour and added, "Good luck, Nancy Drew! Let's hope you or the police find this suspect Roger Hoelt pretty soon!"

With a smile he turned towards the door and left. Nancy dropped into a nearby chair. "This is getting worse and worse," she said. "That man Hoelt is really dangerous!"

Mrs Glick came to Nancy's side and laid a motherly hand on her shoulder. "We will not talk about this any more. Tomorrow you are going to forget the mystery and have a good time. It is market day. Would you girls like to help me stand market?"

"Oh, we'd love to!" cried Nancy, her face brightening. "What can we do for you, Mrs Glick?"

The farm woman said that the vegetables had to be picked after sundown, washed, and arranged attractively that evening for the market. "Then early tomorrow morning we will bake bread and make pies and cakes to sell," she told Nancy.

The family and their visitors had an early supper. Then Mrs Glick and all the girls went into the mathematically precise garden and began picking plump carrots and beets. When their baskets were full, Nancy and the cousins carried them to the sluice for washing. Next, they were sorted into sizes, cleaned, then tied into bunches. Meanwhile, Mrs Glick and Becky were picking other vegetables. By bedtime, all the produce was ready to be taken to town the next morning.

The girls, tired from the long day, quickly tumbled into bed. It seemed they had hardly fallen asleep when Mrs Glick knocked on their doors. "It is four o'clock. Time to get up!" she called to them.

In answer, Bess opened one eye and looked round the dark room, then dived deeper under the covers. George gave a tremendous yawn, turned on to her other side, and went back to sleep. Nancy did not even wake up.

After a while a louder knock came on the doors. This time, Mrs Glick said nothing until the girls answered. Then she called, "Girls, it's four-thirty. If you're going to help me, you must get up now!"

The girls jumped out of bed, hurried into their clothes, and raced downstairs. They found Mrs Glick, with Becky's help, busy with her baking. On a side table stood several boxes of biscuits. From the oven came the aroma of apple pie.

"You are sleepy birds," Mrs Glick teased, while stirring batter for a cake. "But you are in time to make the *fasnachts*."

The hot fat was ready for the willing helpers. One by one, Nancy and George dropped the batter of doughnut rings into it. As soon as each one was cooked, it was removed, dried on paper, and sprinkled with powdered sugar by Bess.

"When you get hungry, help yourselves," Mrs Glick invited. "We will not have time this morning to sit down to breakfast."

The girls waited until they had finished frying the doughnuts. Then they helped themselves to huge slices of buttered bread on which they heaped apple butter. The meal was topped off with *fasnachts*.

"We'll leave at six sharp," Mrs Glick announced, as she bustled about the homely kitchen.

As the clock was striking that hour, the last of the food was being packed into the Glicks' car. Then the farm woman, Nancy, Bess, and George got in and started for town.

When they reached the market, the girls helped Mrs Glick carry her produce to the stall that had been assigned to her. After it was attractively set up, the woman suggested that the girls walk through the market, then look round the town.

"Market day is a big one here," she said. "Many of the people do not come to town at any other time. Everyone always enjoys it."

The girls were intrigued not only by the hearty, appetizing foods and the bright flowers on display, but also by the stalls where hand needlework and cookbooks were on sale. The visitors each bought a book and a colourful apron to take home.

"The plainer the people, the fancier their decorations," Bess commented.

Outside the market, Nancy and her friends watched

Amish carriage after carriage arrive. There was a long row of hitching posts to which the horses were tied side by side. There was not a black horse among them.

"I guess Hoelt wouldn't dare show up in this crowd," George remarked.

Most of the men and women were tall and strong looking. All had good colour and bright eyes.

George suddenly grinned. "The minute they turn their backs, you can't tell one from another!"

Bess giggled. "I should think young men would have a hard time keeping track of their dates!"

An hour later the girls decided to return to the market to see how Mrs Glick was getting along. As they turned the corner they saw an Amish girl coming towards them.

Suddenly Nancy cried out, "Why, Manda Kreutz!"

· 12 ·

Mistaken Identity

As Nancy and her chums stopped before Manda Kreutz on the street, the Amish girl looked at them blankly. She gave no sign of recognition.

Ignoring this, Bess said to her sweetly, "Why did you run away from home again?"

"I think you must have me mixed up with someone else," the girl replied. She started to walk on.

Nancy took her arm. "Surely you remember us—the girls who met you on the road when you were walking home from Lancaster?"

Suddenly the Amish girl smiled. "I guess you have mistaken me for my cousin, Manda Kreutz."

The three girls were stunned. Now that they took a closer look at the stranger before them, they knew she was not Manda. This young woman was slightly shorter and plumper. But otherwise the cousins looked enough alike to be identical twins.

"Well, I certainly thought you were Manda," Nancy said, smiling, and introduced herself and her friends. "We met your cousin the other day and have been trying ever since to find her."

"I'll tell you where she lives," the Amish girl said. "By the way, my name is Melinda Kreutz."

George spoke up. "We know where Manda's family lives, but she is not living at home. Didn't you know this, Melinda?"

"No," the Amish girl replied. Then, looking at the others searchingly, she said, "Is something the matter?"

Bess answered quickly, "You mean you don't know Manda has run away from home?"

"*Sell iss awschrecklich!*" Then Melinda added quickly, "I beg your pardon. You do not understand our language. I mean, it is dreadful. I did not know about Manda, for I do not hear from my cousin often. Our ways are different. I am Church Amish."

After hearing the story, she shook her head. "My uncle is too stern but he loves his family. Soon, though, Manda would have married and gone away from home, anyhow. She should not have run away."

"You mean Manda has wedding plans?" Bess asked.

"No. There was no young man I've heard of. But all Amish girls marry young," Melinda explained.

Melinda was glad that Manda's father had decided to forgive her and take her back. She hoped that Nancy and her friends would soon find her cousin.

"Can you give us any hint as to where she may be?" the young detective asked. "We heard she was working for an Amish couple who have recently moved into this area."

Melinda studied the sidewalk for several moments. Then she looked up and said, "This may help you. Two days ago a man hurried up to me on the street and began to talk. I guess he thought I was Manda."

Nancy asked what he looked like. The girl's description fitted Roger Hoelt in Amish disguise.

"Did he say anything to give you an idea where Manda might be?" George prodded.

Melinda said that the man had rushed up to her and cried out in Pennsylvania Dutch, "You've got to get out of here quick and go back to the *schnitz*! That witch girl is coming!"

Nancy was furious. Roger Hoelt had convinced Manda that Nancy was a witch!

"Please go on, Melinda," she requested as calmly as she could.

Melinda said she had told the man that she did not know

what he was talking about. He had tried to argue with her and had said, "You can't run out on my wife and me like that!"

But when Melinda had still persisted that she did not know him, a frightened look had suddenly come over his face. He had mumbled something about thinking she was someone else and had rushed off.

"What do you think the man meant by his strange words?" Melinda asked Nancy.

Nancy smiled. "I don't know, Melinda. You should know better than I. What is a *schnitz*?"

Melinda said it was a word with variations of meaning, but that it had to do with apples. In recipes such as *schnitz un gnepp*, it meant dried apples and dumplings. A *schnitzing* was an apple paring and drying party.

"Well, how would you interpret what the man said to you about going back to the *schnitz*?" George asked Melinda.

The Amish girl thought it might mean a *schnitzing*. "What I would like to know is who the witch girl is."

"I don't know," Nancy replied quickly. Then the three girls said goodbye and hurried off.

"Well, we picked up a good clue, even though we didn't find Manda," Bess remarked.

"A very good clue," Nancy agreed. "Now we must locate someone who knows where the *schnitz* is." She asked a policeman but he could not help her.

The girls returned to the market and walked among the stalls until they came to Mrs Glick's stand. To their amazement, she had sold nearly everything she had brought from the farm.

"A couple more pie sales and I shall be able to return home," she said, smiling.

"That's great," Nancy praised her. Then she told about the mistaken identity between Manda and Melinda Kreutz. "Do you know where the *schnitz* is?" she asked.

Mrs Glick had never heard of it. "We ask Papa when we

get home," she said. "I'll be ready to leave in about half an hour."

Nancy turned to the other girls and suggested they walk round the town again and keep an eye open for Roger Hoelt. "Evidently he does come into town. I presume he relies on his disguise to keep him from being identified."

The girls were about ready to rejoin Mrs Glick when Bess suddenly spied a black horse and carriage in front of a bakery.

"Look!" she cried. At the same moment a slender Amish woman of middle age came from the shop and got into the carriage.

"Do you suppose that could be Mrs Hoelt?" Bess asked eagerly.

"There's one way to find out," Nancy replied, and dashed into the bakery to ask her identity.

"That was Mrs Esch," the girl behind the counter told Nancy.

"Has she lived here a long time?" Nancy inquired.

"Oh, yes," the clerk said.

Returning to her friends, Nancy sighed and said, "Another false clue."

As the three walked back to the market, Bess again cried out, "Look down the road! There's another black horse and Amish carriage."

The girls rushed towards it. But just as they were almost near enough to see the driver, he started off. The man looked fleetingly in their direction, then slapped his horse, and it galloped off down the road.

"That was the same man who passed us the other day!" George cried. "He's Roger Hoelt! Come on! We must catch him!"

Nancy's first thought was to run to Mrs Glick's car and give chase. But she did not have the ignition key. By the time she could get it, Hoelt would be out of sight.

"I'll report this to the policeman over there," she said, and hurried up to him. Nancy gave the officer the details of the mystery quickly.

"I have orders not to leave my beat," the officer said reluctantly. "I'm sorry, miss. Why don't you go to police headquarters and report your suspicion to them?"

He gave her directions and the three girls hurried off. But suddenly Nancy stopped. Headquarters was still five blocks away and by the time they reached it Roger Hoelt would have pulled off the road and hidden somewhere.

"Let's not report anything," she suggested. "Next time we see Hoelt we'll have more to go on. I hate making a nuisance of ourselves to the police."

Nancy, Bess, and George returned to Mrs Glick, who was sorry to learn that they had missed catching the thief. The group returned home and Nancy at once asked Mr Glick if he had ever heard of the *schnitz*.

The cobbler scratched his head and thought for nearly a minute. Then finally he said, "At one time there was a farm somewhere around here that had an apple-drying business. Maybe it was called the *schnitz*, although I never heard any name for it."

Mr Glick did not know its exact location but would inquire of his neighbours. Nancy drove with him to several farms in the area. No one they asked had ever heard of the *schnitz*.

At each place Nancy also showed the drawing of the witch tree symbol. Since none of these people had ever seen it, she came to the conclusion it was a hex sign used only by Hoelt. He probably had designed it himself.

"Well," she told herself philosophically, "if I ever do come across it on a barn or house I'll certainly expect to find Hoelt there!"

During the evening Mr and Mrs Glick entertained the girls with stories of their younger days.

The three girls slept well and were up early the next morning to continue their sleuthing. It was a beautiful day and they walked outside with Mr Glick for some fresh air before breakfast.

Suddenly the farmer cried out, "*Ach, ya! Waas gayt aw?*"

At the same instant, the girls saw what he was looking at— the witch tree symbol had been painted on the side of the barn!

Underneath it was a picture of a witch riding a broom. No wonder the farmer had said "What goes here?"—the face of the witch bore a strong resemblance to that of Nancy Drew!

·13·

A Disastrous Race

Completely dumbfounded, Nancy, Bess, and George continued to stare at the crudely painted markings on the Glick barn. There was no doubt in their minds that Roger Hoelt or some friend of his had painted the witch tree symbol and the witch riding the broom on the building. It had probably been done by flashlight during the night.

The startling likeness of the witch's face to Nancy's made Bess fearful. "We just can't stay here!" she murmured. "Oh, Nancy, please give up this case. That awful man is getting closer and closer. You're going to be harmed!"

"Sh!" Nancy warned her. "Look at Becky and Henner!"

The two children were standing in the doorway of the farmhouse, frightened expressions on their faces. They whispered to each other, then scooted back into the kitchen.

Immediately Mrs Glick appeared outside. Seeing the marks on the barn, she hurried towards her husband and the girls. None of them had made a comment since Bess's outburst, but now Mr Glick said firmly:

"Your enemy is a very bad and dangerous man, Nancy. He must be made to stop frightening people. There is no room in Amish country for such a person."

Nancy heartily agreed and said that instead of leaving she would double her efforts to locate Roger Hoelt.

"That is good," the cobbler said. "But take care."

. Mrs Glick called her children outside and scolded them for being afraid.

"How many times have I told you there are no witches?"

83

she said sternly. "And to be scared of such a nice girl as Nancy Drew is mean. Come now. Shake hands with her and say you are sorry for running away."

Becky and Henner moved forward obediently, but their approach was timid. Nancy held out her arms to them, suggesting that they help her paint out the silly figures on the barn. Pleased by the suggestion, the two children laughed and ran towards Nancy.

"Can we paint right now?" Henner asked. "I want to paint away the witch."

Nancy looked at Mr and Mrs Glick. The children's father nodded, saying the sooner the figures were removed the better. "No breakfast for the three of you until the picture is all over painted," he said.

Henner said he knew where there was some red paint in the barn because he had been using it on a wheelbarrow the day before. He brought out a can and three brushes, while Mrs Glick provided a ladder for Nancy to use. Then Nancy and the two children started to work.

Bess and George returned to the house with Mrs Glick to help prepare breakfast. In less than half an hour Nancy and the children had finished their paint job, and then everyone sat down to eat.

A few minutes later the telephone rang. Mrs Glick answered it and called Nancy. "It's your father," she announced.

Nancy had sent her father the Glick's address in case he wanted to reach her. She hurried to the phone, worried that something might be amiss at home. But her father's cheery voice reassured her.

"I have to go out of town again, dear, and I thought I'd better let you know. Hannah will go on a short visit to her sister's, unless you're coming right home."

"Dad, I'm sorry to tell you that I'm not getting along very quickly on this mystery," his daughter told him. "So I shan't be home for several days."

"Well, if you change your mind, let Hannah know," the lawyer directed. "By the way, you're going to have company."

"Up here?"

"Yes."

"That's nice," Nancy said. "Who?"

Mr Drew replied that it was to be a surprise for all the girls. His only hint was that some friends of theirs were making a short car trip and would arrive at the Glicks' during the afternoon.

When Nancy returned to the table and told Bess and George about the visitors, they began to speculate at once who they might be. All of them were inclined to think that it was Mrs Tenney and some friends of hers.

"She's getting anxious," said George.

"Yes," Bess added, "Mrs Tenney hasn't heard from you, Nancy, so she's coming here for a report."

"I'm sorry that I haven't a better one for her." Nancy sighed.

After the kitchen had been tidied, Mrs Glick and her children went to weed the vegetable patch. Bess and George offered to help, but Nancy asked to be excused.

"I want to do a little sleuthing round the property to see if I can find any footprints of the person who painted the hex symbol," she explained.

After figuring out which footprints belonged to the Glicks and their friends, Nancy found an unfamiliar set that led from the barn across a field. She followed them for some distance until they came to a road. Here the culprit must have stepped into a car, because the prints ended abruptly and there was evidence that a vehicle had been parked at that point.

With a sigh of disappointment, Nancy returned to the farmhouse. She would have liked to go off in the convertible and do some more sleuthing, but wanted to be on hand to greet the visitors who were coming.

Directly after lunch Bess disappeared and the next time Nancy and George saw her she was dressed in the attractive blue dress she had worn when leaving River Heights.

Mrs Glick, who was with them in the kitchen, smiled. "You must be expecting a young man," she teased.

Bess blushed and said, "Well, one never can tell. In fact," she added, peering out the window, "I had a hunch a couple of hours ago and I was right!"

The other girls rushed to the window. Just pulling to a stop in an attractive cream-coloured convertible were Nancy's boyfriend Ned Nickerson, Burt Eddleton, who often dated George, and Bess's boyfriend, Dave Evans! Delighted, the three girls hurried outside to greet the boys.

"Surprise!" Ned called out, stepping from the car, followed by Burt and Dave.

"Hi!" the other boys and girls called.

"This certainly is a surprise," said Nancy, "and a grand one." Then grinning, she added, "You're just in time to help us solve a mystery."

"That's what we're here for," said Ned, winking. He was tall, with an athletic build, and had brown hair and eyes. "Nancy, your dad has already told me a little about the case. Too bad I was away when it first started."

Nancy's eyes twinkled. "And I suppose Dad mentioned that we haven't had much luck. I hope you've brought us some."

"We sure have."

Burt, who was blond and a little shorter and heavier than Ned, said he would leave the mystery business to them. "I've come up for a good time," he declared with a grin.

"That's a great idea," Bess spoke up, smiling so that her dimples showed.

The group went into the house and Nancy introduced the boys to Mrs Glick. She at once insisted that the new visitors stay there. Ned thanked her and accepted.

"Wait until you taste some of Mrs Glick's cooking,"

George remarked to Dave, a rangy-built, dark-haired young man with green eyes. "You boys will sure have to go into training to make the football team after you leave here."

Mama Glick beamed and blushed a little. "We'll have a very special dinner in honour of your arrival," she told the boys.

Refusing any assistance from the girls, she suggested that they take their friends on a tour of the countryside.

"Then later you can attend one of the gatherings," she told them. "Over at the Stoltz farm they're having a sing-song right after dinner. But maybe"—she smiled—"you would prefer the barn dance at Fischers'."

"I'll take the barn dance," Dave said, and the rest voted for this too.

As the young people drove round the area, Ned became interested in the Amish carriages which passed by. "Suppose you and I go to the barn dance in one of them," he suggested to Nancy.

"All right," she said. "But we'll have to use an open-top one."

"Why?" Ned asked curiously.

"Because all unmarried couples travel that way," she said. "The closed carriages are only for after the wedding."

Ned whistled. "I'll take one of those closed jobs after I graduate. What do you say, Nancy?"

She pretended not to understand and said, "You'll have to give up college and all worldly pleasures if you expect to marry an Amish girl." Ned made a face at her and the others laughed.

Upon returning to the Glick home, the boys met the rest of the family. Ned at once asked Mr Glick if it would be possible to rent a horse and buggy. The man nodded and went to the phone. A few minutes later he reported that he had made the arrangements.

"Drive carefully," he warned, "or you may find yourself the buggy out."

At seven o'clock the horse and buggy were brought to the front door by a young Amish boy. After he had gone, Ned remarked about the peculiar styling of the lad's hair. Nancy told Ned that this was usual among Amish men since all their barbering was done at home. Then she explained quickly about her suspicion that Roger Hoelt was disguising himself as an Amish man. "The shaggy hair and beard are an excellent way to conceal his looks."

Bess and George and their escorts started for the dance in Ned's car, both youths declaring it would be hard to dance after the sumptuous meal they had just enjoyed. "You were right about Mama Glick's cooking," said Burt. "I ate three helpings of *schnitz un gnepp*!"

Ned helped Nancy into the left side of the buggy, then went round and climbed into the driver's seat. He picked up the reins and said "Giddap!" The horse started off at a fast gallop and Ned found he had to keep tight rein to hold the spirited animal in check.

It was a cloudy evening and they had not gone more than half a mile before darkness settled. Ned stopped, got out, and turned on the buggy's lanterns, which worked with batteries.

As they started up again, the horse broke into a brisk trot. Suddenly Nancy and Ned became aware of the sound of galloping hoofs behind them. Turning round, they could dimly make out two buggies, evidently in a race. The drivers seemed to be paying no attention to the buggy ahead of them.

"Oh, Ned!" Nancy cried out. "They'll run into us!"

Ned felt sure that one of the racers would drop behind the other, so there would be no danger of a collision. But he pulled as far over to the right side of the road as he could.

Apparently neither of the rash young drivers behind him was willing to let the other win. Neck and neck, the racers tried to pass Ned's buggy.

The next moment, the wheels of the nearest vehicle

scraped against those of Nancy and Ned's carriage. Frightened, their horse bolted.

The buggy turned over and Nancy was thrown out!

Twenty minutes before the accident, Bess and George and their dates had reached the dance. The Amish young people who had gathered in the barn were very friendly and welcomed the visitors warmly.

The atmosphere was delightfully festive. Lanterns, hung from the rafters, shed a soft glow over the dancers. One young man was playing a mouth organ, another a guitar. The music was very lively and the dancing fast.

After watching the various figures of the square dance being performed, as a man called them out, Bess and Dave swung into one of the circling groups. George and Burt joined hands with another.

"Whew!" said Bess a little later, almost exhausted by the fast side-stepping, twisting, and turning. "Let's sit down for a while!"

"Good idea," Dave panted.

They dropped out, but George and Burt kept going until their particular group finished the set.

When the four met in a corner of the barn, George remarked, "It's strange that Nancy and Ned haven't arrived yet."

Bess giggled. "I suppose they're enjoying the buggy ride."

The words were hardly out of the girl's mouth when an Amish couple rushed excitedly into the barn. They began to speak rapidly in dialect, flinging their arms about as if describing something they had seen.

Curious, George approached an Amish girl standing near her. "What are they saying?" she asked.

"That there was a bad accident," the girl replied. "The witch girl was in it!"

· 14 ·

A Hopeless Hunt

Pushing through the crowd, Bess and George hurried towards the couple who had just arrived at the dance. They were fearful that the injured girl might be Nancy.

"Please tell us in English what happened!" Bess begged the young woman.

"The witch girl—she flew into the air!"

"What! How?" George demanded.

The Amish girl, still agitated, said that her younger brother had been racing the carriage she was in when they saw a couple riding in a buggy in front of them. There was no time to slow down, and as they passed, their vehicle had scraped the wheels of the strange buggy. This had frightened the horse and he had bolted, overturning the carriage. The girl in it should have been badly hurt.

"But she must be a witch because she flew away and nobody saw her again," the Amish girl concluded in an awed tone.

By this time, Burt and Dave had come up. They suggested that the Amish couple try to calm down and tell a sensible story. It was important, because possibly the couple in the carriage were friends of theirs.

The Amish girl tried her best to quieten down, but she was still frightened. Switching from English to Pennsylvania Dutch dialect, it was almost impossible for her listeners to make head or tail of what she was saying. Her partner was of little help.

Finally George said, "What made you call this person who was injured a witch girl?"

"Because she disappeared," the Amish girl replied. "After the accident we stopped our racing horse as soon as we could and looked in the field where the girl was thrown. She wasn't there!"

"I just can't believe it!" said Bess. Then, turning to her cousin, she whispered, "Do you suppose it was Nancy?"

"Since she hasn't arrived here, I'm afraid that it was," George replied grimly. To the Amish couple she said, "There was a boy with this girl. What happened to him?"

"He went *schmaysz muuk*, too."

The young woman's escort said it meant Ned had vanished into the air also.

Now thoroughly alarmed, Bess, George, and their escorts decided that they had better go to the scene of the accident. They must find out just what had occurred and where Nancy and Ned were. Though the girls did not say so aloud, they both wondered whether Roger Hoelt might have been in the vicinity and seen the accident. There was no telling what villainous move he might have made after that.

"Hoelt might even have kidnapped Nancy and Ned while they were stunned or injured!" Bess thought fearfully.

They asked for directions, then hurried off in the convertible. In a short time they reached the field where Nancy and Ned were reported to have disappeared. The open buggy was there, still overturned, but as the Amish couple had said, nothing else was in sight. The young people beamed flashlights over a wide area but saw no trace of Nancy, Ned, or the horse.

"I have a theory," said Burt finally. "I believe Nancy and Ned weren't badly hurt. They probably got up at once and ran after the horse. By the time that Amish couple ran back, Nancy and Ned were out of sight."

"But if Nancy and Ned are all right, where are they? Why didn't they come to the dance?" Bess asked.

Dave spoke up. "If I know Nancy, she returned to the Glicks' to report the accident. Besides, she and Ned probably were a mess from being thrown from the buggy."

The boys' reasoning calmed the girls' fears somewhat. They agreed to go back to the Glicks' and find out if their missing friends were there. But when they arrived at the farmhouse, the group was told that Nancy and Ned had not returned.

Upon hearing the story of the accident and the strange disappearance, the cobbler and his wife became alarmed. "I will call the hospital," Mr Glick offered.

He talked for several minutes with the attendant at the admissions desk, then waited while she checked the hospital's records. At last she told him that neither Nancy Drew nor Ned Nickerson had come in for treatment.

"Maybe the police came by and picked them up in a patrol car," Mrs Glick suggested.

Her husband once more picked up the phone and made the call. The group waited anxiously as Mr Glick asked for the information. Finally he hung up.

"The police do not know anything about the young people or the accident," he said. "I cannot understand what happened to Nancy and Ned."

Bess now voiced aloud her suspicion that Roger Hoelt was somehow mixed up in the affair. Her alarm was infectious and soon everyone in the room was suggesting dire things which might have happened to the missing couple.

Presently Burt stood up. Annoyed with himself for becoming pessimistic, he suggested that all their fears were probably groundless. "Maybe Nancy and Ned stopped somewhere else to freshen up and are now at the dance," he said. "They're probably wondering where we are."

"You have a point there," Dave agreed. "Let's go back to the dance and find out."

Deciding that action was better than sitting round worrying, the girls accompanied the boys. When they reached the Fischer farm, the girls hopped out of the car without waiting for the boys and rushed inside the barn. Bess stepped on to a bench along the wall so that she could look over the dancers' heads. Every couple on the floor was Amish!

"Nancy and Ned are not here," Bess said miserably, as tears of anguish began to fill her eyes. "Oh, George, what are we going to do? I'm terribly worried!"

Just then Burt and Dave, who had been making inquiries among a few couples outside the barn, joined the girls. They held a council of war, but none of them could come up with a suggestion about where to start searching for Nancy and Ned. In despair, the four went outside and climbed back into the convertible. They sat there in silence, each one trying to figure out the problem and how he might help to solve it. Then they decided to drive back to the Glicks', hoping Nancy might have returned there by now.

"I wish," said Bess, as if talking to herself, "that I did have some witchlike powers to see what's hidden from most people's eyes. Then I'd know where Nancy and Ned are."

About three miles away, at this very moment, the missing couple were on a sleuthing mission. Seated astride the horse which Ned had hired for the evening, they were riding along a lonely road in complete darkness. The animal still wore its blinkers and the long reins were looped lightly round the riders. Nancy, seated in front of Ned, held the reins.

A short distance ahead of the two saddleless riders was an Amish carriage being pulled by a black horse. The couple were trailing it, trying to keep from being noticed.

Ned leaned forward and whispered into Nancy's ear, "You're sure that is the stolen carriage with some of Mrs Follett's furniture in it?"

"Yes, I'm sure of it," Nancy whispered back.

"And you feel all right to go on?" Ned asked her solicitously. "Not faint or anything—?"

Nancy assured him she was all right. "I can't miss this chance to nab Roger Hoelt!" she said.

· 15 ·

The Vanished Driver

In silence, Nancy and Ned jogged along on their horse. The carriage they were following, its lights dimmed to the minimum allowed by the law, suddenly turned into a forest road.

"This may be a trick," Nancy warned, "if he knows we're following him."

She pulled gently on the reins to slow their horse's speed and went ahead cautiously. The carriage stopped abruptly. At once Nancy reined in her mount, turned him quickly into the woods, and stopped. She patted his neck soothingly to keep him from pawing the ground or making any other noise.

From among the trees she and Ned could see a light moving along the road. They wondered whether the driver of the carriage was walking back looking for them, or whether he had lost something. As he played the light along the road, the hidden couple hardly dared breathe, they were so fearful of making a sound.

In a few minutes the man turned back and retraced his steps. Getting into his carriage, he started off.

Nancy and Ned, hoping that the hoofbeats of the man's horse would drown out those of their mount, turned back to the road and once more started after the carriage.

"I'm sure that fellow ahead knows he's being followed," Nancy said presently. "He may try something to trap us. We'd better watch our step."

The horse and carriage were some distance ahead now. Suddenly the horse began to gallop. The carriage swayed from side to side and Nancy and Ned expected that at any moment it might turn over.

"That fellow must be crazy to drive so fast," said Ned, "or else he's trying to lose us."

He nudged their horse and it began to run, bringing them closer. After a chase of a quarter of a mile, the carriage stopped abruptly, blocked by a stream of water. The vehicle rocked for a moment but did not go over.

As Nancy and Ned came nearer, the young sleuth again warned about a trap. "We can't tell what the driver's up to."

"You stay here," Ned ordered. "I'll go ahead and find out what's going on."

But Nancy objected. As Ned slid off the horse, she did also. She did consent, however, to stay behind him as they tiptoed forward, using the trees as protection against any sudden attack. But they were not molested and in a few moments they reached the carriage.

No one was in it!

"Say, what's going on here?" Ned asked uneasily, looking round for any watching eyes.

Nancy did not reply to his question. She was listening to detect any sound in the nearby woods which might indicate where the driver was. She could hear nothing but the chirping of crickets.

"Ned," she whispered, "will you stand guard while I examine the furniture in the carriage? I want to be sure that it *is* part of the Follett collection."

"Go ahead," he directed.

The pieces of furniture were small enough for Nancy to lift out herself. One by one, she began to carry them to the carriage lamps and look them over. Although each in turn resembled items on Mrs Tenney's list, there was no way to identify them as actually being the stolen articles.

Disappointed, Nancy had returned all but one piece which she now examined. It was a small hassock with mahogany legs and a petit point fabric top of red roses and festoons of green leaves. Excitedly Nancy realized it fitted the description of a footstool taken from the Follett mansion!

"Ned," Nancy whispered excitedly, "I'm sure we're on the right track. This looks exactly like one of the stolen pieces! And this horse is black like the one Hoelt took! I think both facts are pretty good evidence against him—enough, anyway, to report this to the police."

"Great!" said Ned, but he reminded her that by the time they could get to a phone and report it, the thief might return and take everything with him.

Nancy nodded. "You're right. Then we'll have to take the horse and carriage with us," she said. "You ride our horse and I'll drive the black one."

Ned objected to the arrangement at first. He did not think this was a safe thing for Nancy to do. He still felt that the man who had been driving the carriage was waiting for them in ambush and would prevent them from reporting the incident to the police.

"You could be right, of course, Ned," said Nancy, "but I have a different idea about the whole thing. I think the man who was driving this carriage is not too familiar with these roads. He didn't know about this stream and when he got here he was afraid to cross it in the carriage."

"Sounds logical," Ned conceded. "Too, he probably was afraid of being caught and ran off. He may be a mile away from here by this time. All right, we'll follow your suggestion."

Nancy got into the carriage and urged the horse into a full turn. Then, leading the way, with Ned riding the other horse, she started off.

Though both she and Ned outwardly had shown no fear of what they were about to do, each of them was nervous. It was possible that the man who had left the carriage had gone off for reinforcements. At any moment Roger Hoelt and his assistants might come to claim what they considered was their property! What they might do to the young couple to keep them from going to the police gave both Nancy and Ned some uneasy moments.

But as they reached the end of the forest road, the tension began to lessen. The riders were not stopped. In fact, they met no one on the road.

Nancy, knowing none of the farmers in the neighbourhood and seeing that the lights in the houses had been put out, decided that it would be wiser not to call the police from any of them. She concluded that the best place to go would be the dance. Half an hour later she and Ned reached the Fischers'.

Instead of going to the barn, where the dance was still in progress, Nancy went directly to the house. Getting out, she walked to the door and knocked. By the time it was opened by a smiling, broad-shouldered man, Ned had joined her.

The Amish gentleman invited them into the kitchen. Together, they quickly told their story, and the farmer's face showed his astonishment. Fortunately, he had a telephone and offered to call the police at once.

"They will send a man here in a little while," he reported, after talking with the captain. "It is good that you two found the stolen furniture. But it is too bad that you should miss the dance. Why don't you go over there and make a square? I will call you when the police come."

Nancy smiled and thanked him. She said that after what had happened to her she was more ready for a bottle of liniment than a dance!

"I guess I'm not so hardy as your Amish girls," she added.

The man chuckled. He remarked diplomatically that even an Amish girl, who had been thrown out of a buggy and then ridden for miles bareback, would probably need a massage with liniment, too. He offered to awaken his wife, to give Nancy a treatment, but she said, smiling:

"A hot bath and a good night's sleep will fix me up."

While waiting for the police to arrive, she and Ned talked to Mr Fischer about the farms in the vicinity and Nancy asked him if he had ever heard of a place called the *schnitz*.

"No," Mr. Fischer said. "But I have not lived here very many years. I came from Ohio."

At once Nancy asked him if he had ever heard of a Roger Hoelt from Ohio. But again the farmer shook his head.

At this moment a car stopped at the house and two State Police officers came in. They introduced themselves as officers Wagner and Schmidt.

"You are the couple who may have found some stolen furniture?" Officer Wagner asked Nancy and Ned.

"And a stolen horse and carriage," Ned added.

Nancy told the police about her interview at the carriage factory, and also of hearing that a black horse had disappeared from one of the nearby farms. Officer Schmidt pulled a little book from his pocket and turned several pages.

"Here is a report on both items," he said. "And unless the person who stole the carriage added a final coat of paint to the underside of the right shaft, we may be able to identify the carriage."

The group walked outside. Officer Schmidt took a flashlight from his pocket, got down on the ground, and beamed the light under the right shaft. A smile crossed his face.

"This is it, all right," he said. "The final coat was never put on."

Both officers congratulated Nancy and Ned on recovering the stolen carriage, then looked into the back of it. "What makes you think this is part of the collection of stolen furniture?" Officer Wagner asked Nancy.

She told him about the petit point pattern on the hassock. He smiled and remarked that she certainly was a thorough and discerning detective. Ned was about to tell him more about Nancy's prowess, but she gave him a warning look and he reluctantly kept silent.

"We'll take the horse, carriage, and furniture with us," said Officer Wagner, "and would you like us to return the horse and buggy you rented?"

"Yes, thank you," said Ned, and told where the policemen would find the buggy.

The officers said they would explain to the owner what had happened. Ned asked them to have the man whose buggy had been damaged send him a bill and gave his address.

After the police had gone, Nancy and Ned told the farmer they would go to the dance now and find their friends. They went outside, and for the first time realized that Ned's cream-coloured convertible was not there. They concluded that their friends must have gone back to the Glicks'.

"But how are we going to get home?" Nancy asked.

"Surely somebody here will give us a lift," Ned suggested.

They walked to the barn door and stepped inside. They had no sooner appeared than one of the Amish girls who was dancing stopped short and shrieked. Pointing a finger at the couple, she cried out:

"The witch girl! The witch boy! They've flown back here to hex us!"

The dancing ceased abruptly and the musicians stopped playing. There was a surge of unfriendly looking young men and women towards Nancy and Ned. Fearfully the couple wondered what was going to happen!

·16·

A Hide-out

Weary from the experiences of the evening, Nancy was in no condition to cope with the oncoming hostile group. But Ned instantly took command of the situation.

"Stop!" he cried, holding up his hands.

As the young Amish couples paused, he told them that all the talk about the witch girl was utterly ridiculous. Furthermore, that Nancy Drew might have lost her life because of the foolishness of one of their drivers.

There was silence for a moment, then one of the boys called out, "*Ya*, but I go by the old ideas. This girl makes trouble, ain't?"

"On the contrary," said Ned in a loud voice, so that all could hear him, "Nancy Drew is doing your neighbourhood a favour. She has just found a horse and a carriage stolen from some of your people."

The dancers exchanged glances of amazement. The girl who had made the original statement about Nancy being a witch girl pushed back from the forefront of the group, embarrassed. Ned went on to tell the whole story.

"Nancy is an excellent detective," he stated firmly in conclusion, "but she is not a witch girl. And now, tell us where our friends are. We would like to go home."

There were headshakings among the group, then most of them turned away. The music started and the dancing began again. But several young men approached Nancy and Ned and offered to drive them wherever they wanted to go.

"I am sorry about what happened," one of them said. "We thank you for what you have done."

Ned was just about to accept the offer of a lift when he and Nancy heard the sound of a familiar car engine. Looking outside, they saw Ned's cream-coloured convertible come to a stop. Bess and George, spotting the missing couple, quickly climbed out and rushed over to them.

"Oh, I'm so glad you're all right!" Bess exclaimed, hugging Nancy, and George added, "You scared us out of our wits. We heard you had an accident."

"We'll tell you all about it on the way home," said Nancy, as Ned took her arm and helped her into the car.

Burt and Dave grinned. "Why didn't you two tell us you were going to ride around all of Lancaster County by yourselves on a horse?"

"How were we to know?" joked Ned.

As they drove towards the Glick farm, Nancy surprised the others by saying that she and Ned had actually come to the dance hours before. "You heard about our little accident," she said. "Well, Ned and I chased the horse and caught him. We were so close to the dance that we thought we'd just ride him there and make arrangements to pick up the carriage later.

"After we tethered the horse and were walking to the barn, we noticed an Amish carriage and a black horse some distance away from the others. My curiosity got the better of me and I decided to take a look. No one was in the carriage, but in the back was some furniture that looked like the stolen Follett pieces."

"What!" Bess and George cried in unison.

Nancy smiled. "At least I thought so and later I found out I was right. Well, we waited around to see if Roger Hoelt was in the vicinity. In a few minutes a man came sneaking round the side of the barn, as if he had been spying on the dancers."

"I guess he was looking for you, Nancy," Burt put in. "Was he Roger Hoelt?"

"No. The man came to the carriage, got in, and drove off."

Ned chuckled. "And you know Nancy!" he said. "She decided he was a pal of Hoelt's. And of course she wanted to follow him. So we did!"

He told the rest of the story and the others listened in amazement.

Upon reaching the Glicks', they found that the cobbler and his wife were still up. The couple were overjoyed to see Nancy and Ned and insisted upon hearing the whole story. When it was finished, Mrs Glick said:

"How good that you are safe! And you must be hungry. We will have a little bite to eat. You will all sleep better."

As she started towards the stove, Mr Glick raised his hand. "That is good, Mama," he said. "But first, we will say a prayer of thanks for the safe return of our guests."

The group bowed their heads and he said a short prayer in German. At its conclusion everyone kept his head bowed in silence for nearly a minute. Each, in his own words, added a personal thanks for the safe return of Nancy and Ned. Then, after they had all eaten a hearty midnight snack, everyone went to bed.

After breakfast the following morning, the boys announced that they must leave. Each declared that he had certainly crowded a lot of fun and excitement into the short visit.

"I'm sorry that you can't stay long enough to solve the whole mystery, Ned," said Nancy wistfully. "You've been a big help."

After the girls had waved goodbye to the boys from the lane, they went inside the house to help Mrs Glick with the household chores. As they worked, Nancy remarked that she wanted to start out soon and continue the search for Roger Hoelt.

Mrs Glick's face fell. "I was hoping you would go to Mrs Stoltz's quilting with me," she said. "It is for her daughter."

When Nancy asked her about the "quilting", Mrs Glick explained that an Amish woman spends many years before her marriage making articles for her new home.

"You mean that they know years before whom they are going to marry?" Bess asked, wide-eyed.

The woman laughed. "Oh, no," she said. "But Amish people like to be ready for the future. After a girl is asked in marriage, it is not long before the wedding takes place. She has to have her dower ready." Mrs Glick looked steadfastly at the three girls. "Have you made no preparations for your weddings?"

The girls blushed scarlet and confessed that they had not even thought of a dower. Mrs Glick shook her head sadly. "You should not stay *leddich* too long," she said.

Noting her listeners' puzzled expressions, she translated, "That means not married. Ned and Burt and Dave are such nice *yuung maane*."

"Yes," said Bess, "they are nice young men, but none of us is ready to marry yet."

"You are old enough," Mrs Glick insisted. "You should think about it. Anyway, I want you to go to the quilting with me. You will see what an Amish girl does so that she will have many things ready for her new home."

The girls thought it would be interesting. They said they would stay for a little while at the quilting, then go on their sleuthing trip. An hour later they set off for the Stoltz farmhouse. Mrs Glick drove her own car and the girls went in Nancy's convertible.

At the Stoltz house they found that several women from neighbouring farms had gathered in the parlour. It was explained to the visitors that these were friends and relatives of the family and that they were going to help sixteen-year-old Rebecca Stoltz to make a fancy bedspread.

A large wooden quilting frame had been set up. Stretched taut across it was a white muslin bedspread. Rebecca had just finished cutting out pieces of coloured cloth for the pattern which was to be sewed on the spread. Later, it would be quilted.

Around the edges of the spread was to be a diamond design in bright blue. The centre section would be covered at intervals by big red tulips with green stems and leaves growing out of terra-cotta flowerpots.

Four young women had seated themselves round the quilting frame, threaded needles in hand. Quickly they began to stitch on the blue diamonds, which Rebecca handed to them.

Nancy, Bess, and George were amazed also at the dexterity of the sewers. Not a stitch showed!

The girls stayed for half an hour. Rebecca showed them her dower, which she kept in an old cedar chest. It held several dozen embroidered pillowcases, dressing-table scarves, towels, sheets, and another bright quilt.

Finally, when Nancy told her the girls must be on their way, Rebecca said she would like to give her guests something to remind them of the Amish quilting party. She lifted out a large pillowcase filled with pieces of material in various colours and designs, and gave a large handful of them to each girl.

"You will your own quilt begin, ain't?" she asked, smiling.

Nancy and her chums promised to do this. "We will start patchwork quilts with these," said Bess, and Rebecca nodded contentedly.

After thanking her and saying goodbye to Mrs Glick and the others in the room, the three girls left the house. As they started off in the car, George asked, "Where are we going, Nancy?"

The young detective said she thought that the man who had run away from the carriage the night before had started towards the Hoelts' hiding place. When the driver had realized he was being followed, he had deliberately taken another route.

"What I'm going to try doing," said Nancy, "is figure out at which point he turned off from the direction leading to his destination."

Bess asked Nancy if she had any idea where this was. "I think it may be where the man turned right into the woods road," the young sleuth answered. "When I reach that point, I'll go in the opposite direction."

Driving to the spot, she pulled to the left and followed a narrow road for about two miles. Here it became little more than a footpath. Nancy drove along for a short distance, then decided it was too rough for further progress in the convertible.

"I'm going to park in this field," she said, "and we'll do the rest of our sleuthing on foot."

The path they followed became more and more overgrown and finally ended at a wood.

"Well, this didn't turn out so well," George remarked, as the three peered ahead into the tangled undergrowth.

"The wilder it gets, the more likely it is to be Roger Hoelt's hide-out," Nancy reminded her. "Let's go on."

She set off determinedly through the woods, the cousins following. After they had tramped a quarter of a mile they came to a clearing. Through the trees the girls could see a tumble-down house at one side of it.

"We'd better be careful," Bess warned.

Cautiously, the girls proceeded. They spread out, with Nancy in the middle, their eyes intent on the house.

Suddenly George gasped "Oh!" as her right foot sank into a hole.

A second later, as she tried to wrench her foot free, George found she could not do it. Her whole right leg sank lower.

The next second, all the earth caved in about her and she went down with it!

Investigating a Trap Door

"Help! I'll be smothered!" George called out. The slim girl, terrified, was sinking lower and lower into the hole.

Thoroughly alarmed, Nancy and Bess hurried towards George, but stopped a short distance away. "Careful, Bess," Nancy warned. "We can't help George if we fall in, too. Some of this other ground may be treacherous."

Proceeding with caution, the two girls tested the ground before taking each step. Meanwhile, George kept giving sharp, urgent cries, for she had now sunk up to her waist in the cave-in. The more she struggled, the deeper she went.

"Try to keep calm, George!" Nancy cried. "We'll get you out in a minute!" She turned to her other friend. "Bess," Nancy directed, "lie down on the ground behind me."

While Bess did this, Nancy quickly stretched out full length on her stomach at the edge of the hole. She reached her arms towards George. "Grab my ankles, Bess!" she called again. "When I count three, start wriggling backwards!"

Nancy grabbed George's wrists and said, "Lock your hands over my wrists. Ready!" she called after this was done. "One, two, three!"

Instantly Bess began squirming backwards across the ground. Nancy did the same. But their efforts accomplished little in freeing George.

"Pull a little harder, Bess," Nancy called.

Bess glanced backwards. Almost directly behind her was a small tree. She hooked one ankle round it to give her better leverage. When she and Nancy tried a second time to release George, the pull was more effective. George was heaved a foot out of the pit!

After resting for a moment, the girls repeated the operation. A few more tugs and George was free, sprawled on the ground, a safe distance beyond the edge of the hole. A moment later earth on both sides of the hole fell away.

"Good grief!" she said, panting. "You were just in time! Whew! What a close call!"

The others nodded as they stood up. For nearly ten minutes the girls sat in a circle saying little. George's accident had been a real shock to all of them. Finally she spoke up, asking what the others thought had caused the cave-in.

"I think that there may have been a sluiceway here at one time," Nancy replied. "Probably at this point there was a water wheel and a little dam. Over a period of time it has partially filled in, but the water keeps the ground above it soft."

George, looking at her grimy, splattered clothes, said, "I guess you're right, Nancy. This isn't just dirt—it's mud!" The strong sun, however, soon dried her clothes.

Nancy, who had been thoughtful for some time, suddenly said, "Since nobody came from the house to help us when you cried out for help, George, I guess it's deserted. Let's find out."

"Maybe no one is living in the house," said Bess, "but it may be Roger Hoelt's hiding place. If the stolen furniture is there, he'll probably have it guarded. We'd better watch our step."

The girls advanced cautiously, but no guard came to stop them and there was no response when they knocked on the door.

"I'm sure that the place is vacant," said Nancy, trying the handle. The door creaked open. "Come on in," she added, leading the way.

There was not one piece of furniture in the damp, still house—a one-storey dwelling of three rooms and an attic. In the kitchen ceiling was a trap door to the attic space.

"Another dead end," George remarked, somewhat gloomily. "And I thought sure we'd find something here."

The girls stood still, gazing around the old building and trying to picture life as it might have been lived there fifty years before. Bess was just about to make one of her romantic remarks on the charm of old homes, when they heard a thud in the attic!

"What was that?" she asked nervously, looking upwards.

In answer, Nancy warningly put a finger to her lips. Once more the girls stood in complete silence. Five, ten, fifteen seconds went by. There was not another sound from the attic. Twenty seconds, twenty-five. The girls did not take their eyes off the closed trap door.

When thirty seconds had passed, George whispered, "I guess it was nothing. Let's get out of here, though!"

Nancy shook her head and again put a finger to her lips. Pointing upwards, she indicated that she was going to investigating the attic. Bess, shaking her head and waving her arms, tried silently to dissuade her friend from doing it.

Nancy was determined, however, and motioned for Bess to bend down. The plump girl groaned as Nancy climbed to her shoulders, reached upwards, and tilted the trap door open.

The next second, a shower of dusty newspapers descended on her. Nancy lost her balance and fell to the floor. Bess was bowled over, her eyes full of dirt. Almost at the same instant, a heavy bundle of papers landed squarely on George!

The room was a cloud of dust. Coughing and choking, the three girls made their way out of the cabin to clear their lungs. Bess and George asked Nancy if she had hurt herself in the fall.

"No," Nancy replied, brushing herself off. Then, as a thought came to her, she added, "I don't believe those papers could have tumbled down by themselves."

Instantly Bess became alarmed. "You mean someone was in that attic and pushed them down on us?"

"Yes, I do," said Nancy. "Come on. We're going to find out who it was."

The girls returned to the cabin. There was no doubt that a man had jumped down from the attic. His footprints were clearly evident in the heavy dust.

"He ran out the back door!" George exclaimed, as her eye followed the trail of prints through the kitchen door, which now stood ajar.

"I'm going to follow him!" Nancy said tensely. "Bess, you come with me. George, will you stay here as guard?"

"Sure."

Nancy ran through the back door, Bess at her heels.

George fixed her eyes on the trap door, which was still open. "I wonder if there could be a second person up in the attic," she mused.

In order to find out, she decided to use a ruse. Going to the front door, George slammed in hard, then tiptoed back, peeking round the door to the kitchen. She remained there for several minutes but no one appeared in the opening of the trap door.

"I guess that fellow who ran away was alone," she concluded and went outdoors.

George walked round the house several times but found nothing suspicious. She wondered whether Nancy and Bess had found their quarry.

Presently George's ankle began to throb with pain. Looking down, she noticed it was swollen. "I suppose I twisted it when I stumbled into that hole," she thought.

Dropping to the ground to rest her ankle, George stared absently towards the wood. Presently her attention was arrested by a gnarled old cherry tree before her. From its limbs hung rows of a parasitic whiplike growth, giving the whole tree a weird, grotesque appearance. From where George sat, certain branches crossed in such a way that they resembled a witch on a broom.

"A witch tree!" George exclaimed.

· 18 ·

The Attic's Secret

As George gazed at the strange, bewhiskered tree before her, she wondered if it could have anything to do with the witch tree symbol.

"I'm sure it does," she concluded.

George was rudely aroused from her reflection by a woman's shrill scream. Quickly she turned in the direction from which it had come, but there was no one in sight.

"Could that have been Nancy or Bess?" George asked herself, beginning to worry.

She debated whether or not she should leave her post as guard and try to find out if anything had happened to her friends. Then it occurred to her that the scream might have been uttered by someone else as a ruse to get George away from the old house.

"I'd better stay here," she decided, but continued to worry.

Ten minutes went by. Restless, George began to examine the old tree for any further clues to the mystery. Nothing came to light. Again George looked into the wood. What was happening to Nancy and Bess?

As if in answer to her question, the two girls suddenly emerged from among the trees. Both seemed to be calm and unhurt. When they joined George, she asked if either of them had screamed.

"No," Nancy replied. "It came from an Amish woman in the woods. As we were hurrying along we suddenly saw her in the distance. She screamed and ran off as fast as she could."

Bess took up the story. "We followed the woman but lost her. Nancy and I decided she was probably some farm girl picking berries or wild flowers and that maybe some noise in the underbrush had startled her."

"Did you discover anything?" George asked.

"No," Nancy answered. "We couldn't find the man who was in the attic and decided to come back here to see if you were all right. Any more visitors?"

George shook her head. Then, pointing, she said, "I want you to look at that old tree. If anything ever looked like a witch tree, it does."

The other girls stared at the peculiarly shaped tree for several seconds and agreed. Nancy went over to inspect it, looking in the crotches of the low branches and in a few knotholes for clues.

Finding none as far as she could reach, Nancy shinned up the tree and examined every limb. Finally she descended, reporting that the old tree held nothing which would help them solve the mystery.

"But the witch tree may be tied up with the witch tree symbol," she said. "If so, it could be a landmark for directions to the *schnitz*. Before we leave here, I'm going to investigate the attic and see if there are any clues to the identity of the man who was up there, or to the witch tree symbol."

The girls went back to the house. Again Bess bent over, so that Nancy might pull herself up through the trap-door opening.

"I wish I'd brought my flashlight from the car," Nancy said regretfully.

"I have a tiny one in my pocket," George told her, taking it out and handing it to Nancy.

"Thanks."

Nimbly the young detective hoisted herself through the opening. As she beamed the flashlight round the small attic, nothing was visible except for festoons of cobwebs. Nancy began to brush the strands apart.

After clearing a path towards the far end of the attic, she once more flashed the light around. For a moment she thought there was nothing in it, then her alert eyes picked out a dust-covered object, shoved far back under the eaves. Once more breaking through cobwebs, she crawled over to it.

Quickly brushing off a layer of dirt, Nancy discovered that the object was an old German Bible about ten by twelve inches in size. Its once-beautiful, brown-leather cover was now brittle and frayed.

Before touching the book, Nancy played the flashlight round the rest of the attic to see if she could find anything else. But the Bible proved to be the only object in the old attic. Picking it up gingerly, she made her way to the trap door.

"Bess, will you take this?" she requested. "And be careful of it."

Getting on her knees, Nancy held on to the edge of the opening with one hand and reached down with the other to pass the Bible to Bess. Then Nancy lightly swung herself downwards, holding the rim of the opening with her fingers, and jumped to the floor of the kitchen below.

Bess had already laid the old book on the window sill and was turning back the cover. The flyleaf was brown in spots and speckled from age. Nancy, noticing some faded writing in ink on it, shone her light on the page and read aloud:

" *'Given to Rachel Hoelt by her parents at the time of her marriage.'* "

The girls, touched by the sentiment and amazed by the fact that they had come upon the name of Hoelt, peered at the inscription for several seconds. Then a disturbing thought came to them. Was Roger Hoelt, the thief, a descendant of Rachel Hoelt and her parents who no doubt were devout people?

Finally George voiced her thoughts aloud and added, "Do you suppose this house is still in the Hoelt family?"

"I doubt it," Nancy answered. "If it were, I think the police would have looked here for Roger Hoelt."

Bess suggested that he might have known the house was empty and used it as a hiding place. Then, giving a little shiver, she said, "But I certainly wouldn't want to hide in that dirty old attic."

Nancy said she doubted that this was the real hiding place of Hoelt and his wife, since none of the stolen furniture was here. "Also," she said, "Roger Hoelt had both a car and a horse and carriage. He couldn't drive either of them in here."

George and Bess agreed with Nancy's idea that the witch tree might be a lead to the real hiding place. She was going to continue her search for it!

"Now?" Bess asked. "And what shall we do with this Bible? Put it back or take it with us?"

Nancy said she felt that it would be all right for them to take it along. Some time in the future she would instigate a search for law-abiding members of the Hoelt family who might be interested in obtaining the old book.

"If we leave it here, Roger Hoelt may take it," she said. "And right now I don't think he's the member of his family who should have it. I agree with Bess that he was the man in the attic. Maybe he was looking for the book and we interrupted his search."

The cousins agreed. The Bible was carefully wrapped in some of the old newspapers and carried to the car. Nancy said she wanted to take the old book to the Glicks for safekeeping. "I'll ask them whether this abandoned house is part of a larger piece of property and who owns it now. I have a hunch that we may be narrowing our search for Roger Hoelt and Manda Kreutz."

"Manda may even be back home," George remarked, thinking that by now the Amish girl might have found out that the Hoelts were not the kind of people for whom she wanted to work.

"It's a possibility," Nancy said doubtfully, "though I think we would have heard of it if she had returned to her family. Anyway, let's stop at the Kreutz farm later and see."

Bess was worried. "If she isn't there, I'd hate to have Papa Kreutz go into a rage and throw us out!" she said.

"I'd like to see him try it!" George replied, setting her jaw firmly.

Nancy laughed. "Maybe we can manage to see Mrs Kreutz alone. I don't think she is angry with us, even though her husband is."

By the time they got back to the Glick farm, Mrs Glick had returned from the quilting party. After the girls had changed into clean clothes, they joined the woman in the kitchen. She was bustling about, preparing dinner.

"Um-mm," sniffed George, "something smells mighty good!"

Mrs Glick smiled. "We're having 'old shoes' and *milich flitche*. I have no idea how 'old shoes' got its name," said Mrs Glick, "but I'm sure you'll like the dish. It's mashed potatoes inside of a dumpling. The *milich flitche* is pie. The contents are flour, cream, sugar, and cinnamon."

"Rich," Bess murmured, "but yummy."

Both these dishes proved to be so delicious that again the girls overate. During the meal they told of their morning's experience and asked if Mrs Glick could explain the strange-looking bewhiskered cherry tree they had seen.

"Oh, yes," the woman replied. "The stuff growing on its branches is *hex bayse*. That means witch's broom."

This information made the girls feel even more sure that at last they were pinpointing their search for Roger Hoelt. They told the Glicks of their plan to call on the Kreutzes, to find out if Manda had returned yet.

"I wish you luck," she said, "but don't expect too much. I'm sure if Manda had returned the women at the quilting party would have known about it. And one of them confided to me that the Kreutzes definitely think you are responsible for Manda's vanishing."

Despite this comment, Nancy and Bess started off for the Kreutz homestead. George had begged off because her ankle was bothering her.

As the two girls reached the lane to the Kreutz farm, Bess began to have misgivings and suggested that Nancy drive on and not go in.

"No, I'm going to find out about Manda," Nancy said with determination and drove up to the kitchen door.

No one seemed to be around the barnyard. Nancy and Bess alighted and walked to the door. As they were about to knock, it was opened by Mrs Kreutz. Grabbing each of them by a shoulder, she yanked them inside, crying:

"*Dummel dich!*"

A Clue from Groeszdawdi

Mrs Kreutz quickly closed the kitchen door behind Nancy and Bess and said, "Please to forgive me for speaking in Pennsylvania Dutch to you. I was saying 'hurry'!"

"What's the matter?" Bess asked quickly.

Manda's mother looked all round as if afraid someone would hear her reply. In a whisper she said, "I could not let you stay outdoors. Papa has come to believe you girls persuaded Manda to run away. He has told many people this. If he should drive in now, please run yourselves the front door out."

Nancy felt that she should remind Mrs Kreutz that the convertible parked outside was a dead giveaway. But before she could say a word, Mrs Kreutz asked breathlessly, "Have you news of Manda?"

"We were hoping she might have returned home," Nancy replied. "We haven't been able to find her."

Mrs Kreutz wrung her hands. "Oh, my little daughter!" she wailed. "If it had not been for Papa saying no one could talk to her, she would be here now. I am so afraid she is in danger."

The girls agreed with this but did not voice their opinion. Instead, they assured Mrs Kreutz that they were doing everything possible to find Manda. "The police are trying to find Mr and Mrs Hoelt, for whom we think Manda is working," Bess added.

Nancy brought the girl's mother up to date on all that had

happened, ending with the question, "The man on the street who spoke to Manda's cousin Melinda, said, 'Get to the *schnitz*!' Have you any idea what he meant?"

When Mrs Kreutz said no, Nancy inquired if the woman had ever heard of a storehouse for dried apples in the neighbourhood. At this remark Mrs Kreutz turned pale. Grasping Nancy's hand, she said:

"Manda asked me that very question!"

"I believe that's where she has gone," Nancy said. "Where is the storehouse?"

Sadly the Amish woman admitted that she did not know. She had never heard of such a place.

"If Manda was trying to find it," said Nancy, "where would she go to get information about it?"

Mrs Kreutz replied that there was one very old man in the neighbourhood who might be able to help. "He knows about everything that took place long ago," she said. "I have never heard of any new storehouses, so this place must have been used years ago."

"Who is this man and where does he live?" Nancy asked eagerly.

"He's Groeszdawdi Esch," Mrs Kreutz answered. "He lives in one end of a three-generation house."

Bess wanted to know what this was, and Mrs Kreutz explained that in Amish country families rarely separate. Sometimes a man will build a house on part of his property for a son about to be married. "Other parents," she said, "build a wing on to the main house, and the father and mother move into it when one of the sons marries."

"And where does the third house come in?" Bess asked.

Mrs Kreutz said it was hard to explain this in English. Anyway, there were three houses attached, each smaller than the one beside it. In the smallest house lived the grandfather, in the centre building was the father, and in the largest house was the grandson and his family.

"Groeszdawdi Esch lives in the smallest house," she said. Pointing in a northwesterly direction, she added, "If you could fly like a crow, you would hit on it."

"I'm sure we can find it," said Nancy. "And now we had better go before your husband returns."

Mrs Kreutz quickly agreed. He had gone to a cow sale to sell the ugly bull which had attacked him, but he probably would be home any minute. The girls hurried outside, climbed into the car, and drove off.

They found the Esch farm with little trouble. As they reached the barn they were surprised to see a dozen Amish carriages assembled. "There must be a party going on," said Nancy.

At that moment a young boy, carrying a bucket of apple parings, came dashing from a small stone building. He dumped the contents of the pail into the pigsty.

"I'll bet this is an apple *schnitzing*," Bess remarked.

Realizing that Groeszdawdi Esch and everyone else on the farm would be in the kettle house, Nancy and Bess got out of the car and went directly there.

"Doesn't it smell heavenly!" said Bess as she sniffed the spicy aroma coming from the building.

Nancy and Bess stepped inside and watched the busy scene with fascination. Seated on chairs and apple crates were several men and women, old and young. Each one held a metal, box-shaped apple parer on his lap. It worked with a quick turn of the handle and took off the skin of the apple in a jiffy. Next, the fruit was cored and put into large kettles, which were lifted into a warm oven. Here the moisture would be baked out of them.

Several minutes passed before the girls were noticed. Then a young woman left her work and came over to ask if she could be of assistance to them. Nancy stated that she had come to talk to Groeszdawdi Esch.

"I will get him," the woman offered.

Presently an elderly man with snow-white hair and beard

approached them. He had kindly blue eyes, and despite his advanced age was tall and erect.

The old man smiled pleasantly at the visitors. "Groeszdawdi can help you?" he asked.

Nancy explained that she was looking for a place known as the *schnitz*, which she thought was an old-time dried apple storehouse.

"*Ach, ya*," the man said. "I know the place. A long time ago it belonged to a farmer named Hoelt."

Nancy could hardly conceal her excitement. "Yes, go on," she urged.

"The Hoelts have not lived there for a long time," Groeszdawdi went on. "They sold the place to city people named Fuller. But now they have abandoned it."

"Why?" Bess spoke up.

Groeszdawdi Esch looked first at one girl, then the other. "Before I tell you, explain why you want to know about it."

Nancy wondered what was behind the elderly man's question, but she replied that Manda Kreutz was missing, and that she had a clue Manda might be hiding at the *schnitz*.

"*Gfaiirlich! Ess iss wie toedt!*"

The girls waited for Mr Esch to translate. In a moment he did. "It's dangerous! It's like death!"

He went on to say that if Manda were there, she, too, might vanish mysteriously as many others had on that farm.

"But why?" cried Nancy. "Tell us so that we can save her!"

Groeszdawdi Esch shook his head and wagged a finger at the girls. "Stay away from that spot! It is bad luck—very bad luck!"

·20·

The Gypsy's Story

Would Groeszdawdi Esch refuse to tell them where the *schnitz* was? Nancy and Bess wondered. Since he had pronounced it a dangerous place from which people had disappeared, it was unlikely that he would reveal its location.

Nancy, however, finally persuaded him to tell her where the place was. He hesitated a long time, then finally said, "Go four miles north from here. You will see a lane running through a field that has not been tilled for years. The road is overgrown and rutted. Nobody uses it, but you can't miss it, if you keep your eyes open."

. On a hunch Nancy asked whether there was another house on the property some distance from the main building. Groeszdawdi Esch nodded, saying that the old Hoelt family had several children. The father had built houses for them in various locations on the property.

"Was one of the women named Rachel Hoelt?" Nancy asked.

The old man looked at her searchingly and asked how she happened to know of a Rachel Hoelt, who had died fifty years before. Nancy said that she had seen an old Bible with the name in it.

"That's the farm," he said. "But I'm telling you again, stay away from it!"

"Why is it dangerous?" Bess spoke up.

The old man took a deep breath, then began his story. He used so many Pennsylvania Dutch words and phrases with his English that it was difficult for the girls to understand him. But after they had questioned him several times, Nancy and Bess finally got the gist of the tale.

A long time ago, Groeszdawdi Esch related, when the Hoelts lived on the farm, some members of their family vanished mysteriously and were never seen again. Neighbours concluded that there was a hex on the family. One day a band of gypsies came along and set up their tents on the property.

"Old Mr Hoelt was furious," Groeszdawdi said. "He was sure the gypsies would bring him even worse luck. He ordered them away, but they only moved to a wood on his property."

It seemed that old Mr Hoelt was not aware of this, but several of his children went to the encampment and became friendly with the gypsies. One of the women was a beautiful, young fortune-teller. Mr Hoelt's eldest son and she fell in love and planned to marry.

The old man found out and stopped the marriage by threatening to disinherit his son. The fortune-teller was furious. She told him that she knew the secret of why members of his family had disappeared, but she would never tell him unless he consented to the marriage. It was a terrible choice for the old man to make, but he decided to keep his son at home.

Later, people said that the gypsy woman out of love for the young man had left him a clue to the secret. She had written it down in English on a piece of paper and hidden it in a table which she had left behind for her beloved. Rumour had it that this table somehow had been acquired by the gypsies from the collection in George Washington's home.

As Groeszdawdi Esch finished the story, Nancy and Bess glanced at each other. Was this the table for which Roger Hoelt had been searching?

Mr Esch told the girls that the present owner of the property, Mr Fuller, had also had bad luck on the farm. No one in his family had disappeared, but his cattle had become ill and died, he had had poor crops and several accidents, and illness had hounded the family.

"Who is operating the farm now?" Nancy asked.

"No one," the old man replied. "The Fullers have left there, but they have not put the property up for sale. I do not know whether they intend to come back."

Nancy concluded that this might explain why Roger Hoelt and his wife had chosen this particular place in which to hide. He was trying to find out what the secret was. Should he discover it, and the answer was something that might bring him a lot of money, he no doubt would offer to buy back the property.

A faraway look came into Groeszdawdi's eyes. Then he said, "You say that maybe Manda Kreutz is hiding on the Fuller property?"

"I'm afraid so," Nancy answered. "I'm going to go there and try to find her. Have you any idea what makes the place dangerous, so I could avoid any trouble?"

The old man said it was a mystery to him and that he had never heard anything to give him the slightest clue as to what the secret was.

"But the few people who know the story avoid the place like the plague!"

Nancy thanked Groeszdawdi Esch for his information and promised to be very careful in her search. He smiled and said he hoped that Manda would be safe at home soon and that her papa would not be too harsh with her.

"Manda is pretty and she is a good worker," he said. "She will soon get a husband and her papa will not have to worry," he added, chuckling.

The girls chuckled too, recalling that Melinda had said the same thing. They said goodbye and left.

Nancy wanted to start immediately for the Fuller farm, but Bess protested. "Nancy Drew, after all you've heard, you're going to go there?"

"Yes."

"Well, you'll take somebody except just me," she announced firmly. "We'll collect George and half a dozen other people."

Nancy laughed. "Where are we going to get all these people?"

Bess said she did not know but they were not going alone. The girls continued to discuss the matter as they drove off.

"You're hinting that I call in the police, Bess," said Nancy. "I don't want to do that. We haven't one definite thing to go on. Dragging officers out on what may be a wild-goose chase wouldn't be right.

"What I propose to do is to find out whether Mr and Mrs Hoelt are really hiding at the Fuller farm. And if Manda is there working for them, I want to get her away before I call in the police. We don't want Manda to get any bad publicity."

Bess finally conceded that Nancy was right. "But it's getting late in the day. I won't hear of your going until tomorrow morning."

"All right," Nancy agreed.

Presently she remarked that it was likely the furniture thief and his wife were using Manda as a front. So far as the Amish girl knew, the couple were honest. "Manda has led a sheltered life," said Nancy. "She would probably believe any story the Hoelts might tell her and pass it on to any unexpected visitors."

"Of course the unexpected visitors aren't supposed to include you and George and me," said Bess. "Roger Hoelt tried to brain us in that little cabin. No telling what he'll do if we show up at his real hide-out."

Nancy did not comment on this remark. Instead, she said, "I'm convinced now that the woman who screamed in the woods and ran away was either Manda or Mrs Hoelt. With the Amish-type head covering, it's hard to distinguish faces at a distance.

Bess's face took on a worried look at once. She suggested

that the secret danger connected with the property might have caused the woman to scream. "Maybe it's some kind of a witch or other hex," she murmured.

"It probably was only a snake," said Nancy.

At the Glicks' farm, Nancy and Bess related their latest news. The children and their parents were intrigued.

"What is a gypsy like?" Becky asked. "And how do you tell fortunes?"

Her mother explained, then said, "There is no more sense to fortune-telling than there is to hexing. Now we will talk no more about nonsense."

The visitors took the cue, changed the subject, and later helped Mrs Glick with preparations for supper. Glancing outside, Nancy saw Becky and Henner playing in the barnyard.

As she watched, the little boy raised a slingshot. Nancy was amazed that his parents would let him use this dangerous plaything. Henner was very proficient and could make a stone whistle through the air a long distance.

'Henner would make a good hunter," Nancy remarked to the boy's mother. "He has a very accurate aim with his slingshot."

Mrs Glick agreed, but said that once in a while he became erratic and hit something he had not intended to. "But he is improving every day," she said.

Directly after supper the three girls took a walk and discussed the mystery again. They had just started back to the house when Mrs Glick called to them.

"Telephone call for you from home, Bess," she said.

Bess hurried into the house. The other girls followed, thinking that there might be some news for them too.

As they stepped through the door, Bess was saying, "Hello!" She listened for a few seconds, then hung up.

Suddenly Bess burst into tears!

A Slingshot Strikes

"Bess, what happened?" Nancy cried, rushing to her friend's side and putting an arm about her. "Is it bad news?"

Bess stopped sobbing and said in a quivering voice, "Nancy dear, I hate to tell you this, but it was your father's secretary calling. Oh, Nancy, I don't know how to break such news."

Nancy's heart began to pound. "Tell me, whatever it is," she begged.

Finally Bess said that Mr Drew was dangerously ill in a hospital and it was doubtful that he would recover. "He keeps calling for you all the time, Nancy," Bess went on. "Everybody thinks you should come home at once."

Nancy had turned chalk white. She was completely stunned—too stunned even to shed a tear. Like someone in a trance, she turned towards the stairway, saying she would get her car keys and leave at once. Bess quickly said she would go along.

Mrs Glick hurried to Nancy's side. Putting a motherly arm around the girl's waist, she told her how sorry she was to hear the unfortunate news.

Mr Glick had arisen from his chair. He also came to Nancy's side to offer his sympathy. "You should not be driving all night," he said. "Anyway, it would be faster for you to fly. I will telephone the airport to see about a plane and drive you over there."

Nancy thanked him, agreeing that would be the best way for her to get to River Heights in a hurry. She only hoped she would not be too late to see her father alive.

All this while George had remained silent. It was not because of lack of sympathy, but it had occurred to her that the whole procedure was most irregular. If Mr Drew were so ill, Hannah would have returned to River Heights and called Nancy direct. Or, her own or Bess's parents would have been in touch with the girls.

The more George thought about it, the more suspicious she became that the telephone call might have been a hoax. Mr Drew's secretary, she knew, had been in the lawyer's employ only a short time and Bess had never spoken to the girl. So she would not have been able to identify the voice. For this reason, it would be very easy for someone else to pretend to be the secretary.

"Mrs Glick," said George, "did the operator tell you the call was from River Heights?"

"Why, no," the Amish woman replied. "It was the secretary herself I talked to."

"That's not the usual way a long-distance call is made to an outlying area like this," George reminded the others. She now told them her suspicions and suggested that a call be put in to the Drew home. If there was no answer, she would try her own house.

Nancy had paused on the stairway. Her heart leaped with hope! George's idea was a very good one. Nancy prayed the girl was right about the hoax!

Everyone waited breathlessly while George placed the call to the Drew house. There was no answer. Nancy relaxed a little. This must mean that Hannah Gruen was still visiting her sister! But George wasted no time in trying her own home. Less than a minute later she was saying hello to her mother, and adding, "Is it true that Nancy's father is in the hospital very ill?"

"Why, absolutely not!" Mrs Fayne answered. "I was speaking with Mr Drew only five minutes ago. He was leaving for an overnight business trip."

"Hold the line just a moment, Mother," said George. She

turned and relayed the good news to everyone. Nancy's eyes filled with tears of joy and relief. She was sorry not to have spoken with her father. He had probably just missed the telephone call. George resumed talking with her mother, telling about the fake message.

"Why, how dreadful!" exclaimed Mrs Fayne.

"It's wicked," said George. "Nancy almost has the mystery solved. The furniture thief is up here. It was a pretty cruel method for him to use to get Nancy out of this area."

Mrs Fayne felt that in view of what had happened Nancy should not pursue the case any longer.

"Mother, you know how Nancy is," George replied. "She won't give up!"

"I suppose not," George's mother replied. "But do tell her to be careful, and you and Bess watch your step too."

George promised to do so, then hung up. Nancy came down the stairs and hugged George. She praised the quick-witted girl for realizing the call might be a fake.

"Mrs Roger Hoelt got the better of me that time," she said ruefully.

Nancy and the other girls, weary from their long day and the fright they had just had, went to bed early. All of them wanted to be fresh for the exciting detective work ahead of them.

The following morning, the girls were downstairs even before Mrs Glick appeared. Not knowing what she had planned for breakfast, they walked outside. Nearby, Henner was practising with his slingshot.

"Whom are you shooting now?" George asked him playfully.

"Goliath," the little boy answered. "I'm David."

The girls laughed, but Henner did not. He said he was perfecting his aim, so that if any bad people came around to bother Nancy, he could use his slingshot as David had.

"Oh, Henner, you mustn't have such ideas," said Nancy.

"If any bad people come around here, you let your dad handle them."

Henner was not convinced. He insisted that he was bigger than Nancy realized and was old enough to help if anything like that should happen. Nancy said no more on the subject. Deciding to pick some flowers for the breakfast table, she wandered off to the garden.

She had just gathered a large bouquet when suddenly she heard Bess shriek, "Look out!"

Nancy started to turn to find out what Bess meant. She was too late. At that moment something hit her in the back of the neck and she slumped to the ground, unconscious.

Bess was at her friend's side almost immediately. "Oh, Nancy!" she wailed. Behind her, Henner was saying, "I didn't mean to do it. Is Nancy bad hurt?" The little boy dashed over to the girls.

By this time, George had also run up and together she and Bess carried Nancy into the house and laid her on a sofa. Mrs Glick, who was just coming downstairs, rushed to find out what had happened.

"I did it, Mama!" Henner cried. "Oh, Mama, maybe I've killed Nancy with my slingshot."

Before his startled mother could calm the small boy, Henner hurried up the stairs, weeping. Mrs Glick immediately turned her attention to Nancy.

"This is dreadful," the woman said.

She inquired where Nancy had been hit with the stone, and upon learning it was in the back of the neck, said at once, "We must quick get the doctor!" She made the call, then returned to Nancy. She took hold of one of the girl's hands and began to murmur a prayer. Bess, meanwhile, had wrung out a cloth in cold water, which she now placed on Nancy's forehead. George began chafing her friend's wrists.

Nancy slowly regained consciousness but was still groggy when the doctor arrived twenty minutes later. He said that fortunately Nancy had received only a glancing blow, judging by the scratches on the back of her neck. The doctor assured her friends that she would be all right, but should be quiet the rest of the day.

When Nancy's mind cleared, she smiled wanly and asked what had happened to her. George related the details of the accident.

Henner, meanwhile, had quietly come downstairs. "Poor Henner!" Nancy remarked. "Please don't punish him, Mrs Glick. He meant no harm."

Mrs Glick said she felt sure her son had learned his lesson but that she would take away the boy's slingshot. A few minutes later the doctor said he was sure Nancy would suffer no ill effects from the accident and that he must be going.

"I want you to rest today, Miss Drew. Don't even do any walking around—stay on this sofa until bedtime," he ordered.

He left at once, giving Nancy no opportunity to object. When she sadly mentioned having to postpone her sleuthing, Bess spoke up.

"Finding Roger Hoelt isn't worth risking your health," she said sternly. "Nancy, if you try to get off that sofa, I'm going to tie you down."

Nancy smiled softly. At the moment she entertained no such thought. In fact, going to sleep was the only thing which appealed to her. For the rest of the day, Nancy dozed a good deal and ate lightly. She went to bed early in the evening. To her own and everyone else's relief, she felt fine the next morning and ready to resume the search for Manda and her thieving employers, the Hoelts.

As soon as breakfast was over, Mrs Glick playfully shooed the girls out of the house. They headed for the convertible. To their surprise, the car was not in its usual place by the barn.

"Did one of you move it yesterday?" Nancy asked.

The cousins shook their heads. "Maybe Mr Glick put the

car in the barn," George suggested. But this was not the case.

Then the girls went to the little stone building near the barn, where Mr Glick had his cobbler's shop. They asked the kindly man where the convertible was.

"I, too, have wondered," he replied, "but I thought one of you girls had moved it."

Nancy, Bess, and George frantically searched everywhere, but the convertible was nowhere on the Glick farm.

"It's been stolen!" Bess cried out.

· 22 ·

Wheel Off!

The full import of Bess's words dawned on Nancy and George. There was no doubt, they realized with despair, that Nancy's convertible had been stolen!

"You've been hexed again," Bess added dolefully.

"Whether it was a hex or not, it's certainly bad luck," Nancy agreed. "I'll bet Roger Hoelt is responsible for this. He didn't get me to leave last night, so he thought of another trick. Without a car it will be more difficult for us to find his hide-out."

"But that isn't going to stop you, is it?" George asked at once.

"Of course not!" said Nancy, tossing her head vehemently. "It gives me an even better reason for finding him. I'm sure that my car is at the Hoelt hide-out."

"Why not rent another one?" Bess suggested.

Nancy said it was an excellent suggestion, but first she would notify the police. It was possible that the car thief was not Roger Hoelt but a local prankster. If so, the police might easily locate the convertible. It might even have been abandoned on some nearby road.

By now, all the Glicks had assembled and were aghast to hear the story. Henner felt particularly bad that Nancy was having more trouble. He shyly took one of her hands in his own.

"Nancy," he said, "to make up for what I did yesterday I want to help you now."

The little boy had such a pleading look in his eyes that

Nancy gave him a loving hug. "I'll try to figure out how you can assist me," she replied.

Henner said that he already had an idea. His face brightened as he said that it was not too far to the *schnitz*. "I'll drive you there with our horse and carriage," he said.

"That might be a very good solution," Nancy said, smiling. "But first I'll report the theft."

She hurried into the house and called State Police headquarters. Within half an hour an officer arrived and took down all the data. He also made an inspection of the area where the car had been parked.

Presently the officer picked out a set of footprints intermingled with several others, which he declared were those of a man wearing non-Amish-type shoes. "Have you any idea to whom they might belong?" the trooper asked Nancy.

Nancy hesitated. "I can only make a guess," she replied. "I think to Roger Hoelt, about whom you already know. I suspect that he's somewhere in this area and is trying to prevent me from locating him."

The officer said that he would add the theft incident to the list of suspicions against Roger Hoelt. As he stepped into his car, he promised to get in touch with Nancy as soon as he had a lead on her stolen convertible.

The family had breakfast. Afterwards, Mrs Glick said the girls were to do no more housework. "You have too much on your minds already," she stated firmly.

Nancy began to grow restless after another hour had passed by and no word had come from the State Police. Finally she said that with Mrs Glick's approval, she would like to accept Henner's offer of driving to the *schnitz* in the carriage.

"Of course," said Mrs Glick. "And I shall also go with you. It may be dangerous and you should have an older person along. If Papa did not have to be so careful since his accident, I would ask him to go."

"I'll be there, ain't?" Henner exclaimed. "I'll protect everyone! I'm strong!"

His mother looked at him for several seconds, apparently debating whether the boy was old enough to accompany them on what might be a hazardous mission. Finally she smiled. "You are getting to be a big boy. I believe you might help us. Yes, Henner, you may go."

Henner whooped with delight and dashed from the house to hitch up the horse. Within ten minutes he was calling to his passengers. Becky followed the group outside with a wistful expression. Her mother had already laid out some work for the girl to do. "And besides," Mrs Glick said, "you must fix a good lunch for Papa, Becky."

George and Bess got into the rear seat of the carriage. Henner took the reins, with his mother alongside of him and Nancy on the left end. They followed Groeszdawdi Esch's directions.

Soon they reached a side road, which was full of ruts, and the carriage settled into a deep one. The horse plodded along at a snail's pace. About five hundred yards farther on, the road took a sharp turn to the left.

Henner guided the horse round the corner, but in so doing forgot about the rut, which did not turn in their direction. The front wheels pulled out of the rut and settled into another pair of carriage tracks. The rear wheels remained in the former rut. At this instant a rabbit leaped in front of the horse. Frightened, the horse sprang upwards, giving the carriage such a hard jerk that the left wheel came off.

Mrs Glick had helped her startled son rein in the horse by the time the carriage had settled in a tilted position on the road.

"So *druzzel*!" Mrs Glick cried, as everyone got out to survey the damage. Henner, feeling he was again to blame, began to cry. His mother comfortingly said she doubted that the accident could have been avoided. "This is a dreadful road!" she exclaimed.

After examining the wheel, Mrs Glick announced that it would be impossible for them to put it back on the carriage—it was a job for a wheelwright.

"What are we going to do?" Bess asked.

Mrs Glick looked thoughtful for a few moments, then said that the Beiler farm was just across the fields. Turning to Nancy, she suggested that she and Henner ride the horse over there and try to borrow a carriage.

"Henner," his mother said, "you know Michael Beiler in school. I'm sure his family will help."

"*Ya*," replied the small boy, and began to unhitch the horse. When this was done, he and Nancy got on to the animal's back and started off.

It was a mile's ride across the fields to the Beiler farm. Coming in sight of it, Nancy and Henner noticed many carriages-and people around. Uprights for a new building were being put in place.

"It is a barn-raising," Henner explained. "Michael's papa had a bad fire and a barn burned down."

Then, proudly, Henner went on to say that in Amish country neighbours always helped one another to erect new buildings. "This way we are the money in," he said. "And a barn-raising is fun. Everybody gets a lot to eat."

There was a great bustle of activity in the Beiler barnyard. Some of the Amish farmers were bringing up lumber, others were lifting beams into place. In the short time since Nancy had first noticed the barn-raising from the fields, a great deal of construction had been done.

"It will be ready for the floor by dinnertime," said Henner, jumping to the ground.

Nancy also alighted from the horse and tried to get several different workers' attention. But everyone seemed to be too busy to tell her where she might find Mr Beiler.

As she wondered where Mr Beiler might be, Nancy saw that Henner had spied Michael Beiler and run up to see his playmate. Just then one of the workers cried out:

"Heist nus!"

Nancy watched, fascinated, as several of the men began to hoist a heavy beam with their hands. But the next moment her interest changed to a look of horror. The beam tipped, slipped from the men's grip, and began to fall directly towards Henner and Michael!

· 23 ·

Another Hex

With lightning speed Nancy dashed forward to Henner and Michael. Fortunately, the falling beam hit a crosspiece, slowing its descent. The momentary pause gave Nancy a chance to push both boys out of the way and jump to safety herself.

The youngsters sprawled flat on the ground just as the beam crashed to the earth behind them. Bewildered, they scrambled up and looked around. Suddenly Henner realized that Nancy had saved their lives.

"Oh, Nancy," he cried out, "you kept us from being dead already yet!"

"Thank you! Thank you!" Michael exclaimed.

By this time, several of the workers had left their posts and rushed towards the three. In both English and Pennsylvania Dutch, they praised Nancy for her quick action.

One man separated himself from the group and stepped forward. "I am Mr Beiler," he said. "I told my son not to come near the building. I thank you for saving him."

Mr Beiler added that Nancy was no doubt a stranger in the neighbourhood and asked her name. She gave it, then stated her reason for coming to the farm. Mr Beiler replied that he would be very glad to lend her his carriage.

He said that after the barn-raising was over he and his sons would repair the broken carriage, and the following day return it to the Glicks.

"You're very kind," said Nancy gratefully. "I don't want

138

to interrupt the work here. Could Henner and Michael hitch up the horse?"

As they talked, Nancy noticed a woman coming towards them from the house. When she walked up, Mr Beiler introduced her as his wife.

Tears came to the woman's eyes when she learned that Nancy had saved the lives of her youngest boy and of Henner Glick. Smiling at Nancy, she said, "You are a brave girl. Please let me show my appreciation. In the kitchen we are getting ready a big dinner to serve to the men. I want you and Henner to eat some of it."

Nancy thanked her and said she must hurry back to Mrs Glick and the friends she had left on the road. But she did walk to the kitchen with Mrs Beiler while the boys got the carriage.

Nancy had never seen so much food in one house! It seemed to her that there was enough food to feed a small army. On the table were dishes piled high with the traditional "seven sweets and seven sours" which the Pennsylvania Dutch housewife serves at meals. At least fifty moon pies were on trays at one side of the kitchen, waiting to be baked. On the floor stood crocks of *fasnachts*, fried chicken, and pickle relish.

Mrs Beiler, after casting her eye about and introducing several friends who were helping her, picked up a large angel-food cake with whipped-cream frosting.

"Please take this," Mrs Beiler requested. "I will wrap it for you."

She also insisted upon giving Nancy several pieces of fried chicken, a dozen doughnuts, and a jug of lemonade. At this moment Henner drove up to the door and the food was carried to the carriage. Nancy thanked Mrs Beiler once more, then climbed into the wagon, and the young driver turned towards the field over which they had come.

When he and Nancy reached the others, who were

beginning to worry, Henner immediately told them about the falling beam. His mother's eyes opened wide and she put an arm around Nancy's shoulders. With a catch in her voice, she said, "I must admit that I never thought any women were so brave as the Amish. But you have made me see that a girl does not have to be brought up like a pioneer to be courageous and helpful to others."

Nancy flushed at the compliment. Then she showed the food Mrs Beiler had sent and everyone stared in astonishment at the huge quantities. Bess insisted that they take time out to eat and no one else had to be persuaded. All of it was as delicious as it looked, especially the cake which Mrs Glick declared must have contained two dozen eggs!

"And the beating of them surely took an hour," she added.

As soon as they finished eating, they started off once more. This time Mrs Glick, an experienced driver, took the reins. They kept to the fields, crossing several narrow roads. Finally Nancy said that according to Groeszdawdi Esch's directions, they were nearing the old Hoelt farm where the *schnitz* was.

"Do you think we should leave the horse and buggy and walk the rest of the way?" Mrs Glick asked Nancy.

After a moment's thought Nancy said that if Roger Hoelt were on the property he probably had it guarded and already knew they were coming. "I doubt that it would do any good to try hiding the horse and carriage," she said. "And if he isn't there, it will be better to have them with us. We may as well drive right up to the place."

They went on. Skirting a small wood, the searchers suddenly came upon a long, low, dilapidated wooden building. Mrs Glick reined in the horse and stopped.

"This must be the old apple storehouse," she commented.

The others gazed at it. There was no sign of activity round the building, but they had an uneasy feeling that someone might be hiding inside. They all wondered if this was the place where the stolen furniture was stored.

"We'll start our search," Nancy announced. "I suggest that we divide forces. Bess and George, suppose you go in one direction and the Glicks and I will take another."

Bess did not like to see the group split up, but finally agreed that it was the most practical plan.

"But not until we all go into that storehouse together and look around," she said firmly.

Nancy led the way. She pushed open a creaky door and the group entered the lower floor of the two-storey building. Through the cracks between the wide boards enough sunlight filtered in so that they could plainly see the interior. There was one large room—completely empty!

Cautiously, Nancy and her friends climbed to the first floor. The situation here was the same. To convince herself that there were no secret cupboards or other hiding places, the young detective made a thorough search but found nothing.

"There must be a house and barns on the property," she said. "Let's find them."

Outside, the group separated. Bess and George cautiously made their way along the edge of the wood, planning to skirt it completely. Nancy, Mrs Glick, and Henner decided to drive the carriage across the clearing and along a lane which ran through the wood.

At the far end of the wood they came to the yard of the farmhouse. As the three alighted from the carriage, Henner suddenly gave a cry of fright and pointed.

Ahead of them was a witch tree! And painted on it was half of the now-familiar hex sign!

"Look!" Henner shrieked.

A hand, holding a paintbrush, was just reaching round the tree. No other part of a human body was visible. The watchers stared in astonishment at the weird sight.

Henner clung to his mother's skirts. Mrs Glick looked grim and Nancy's spine tingled. For a brief second she felt as if she were seeing a ghostly apparition. Then she brushed this thought aside and dashed forward to see who was behind the tree.

Fully expecting the person to be Roger Hoelt, she was amazed to find a stout, dull-looking boy about sixteen years old. He stared at the girl stupidly.

"What are you doing?" she cried. "And who lives here?"

The youth continued to gawk at her and did not answer. Mrs Glick, who had run up, began to question him in Pennsylvania Dutch. But he did not utter a word and looked as if he failed to comprehend what she was saying.

Suddenly Nancy had an idea. Perhaps the boy was a deaf mute! She decided to test him.

While Mrs Glick was trying to get the boy to talk, Nancy quickly kicked a large stone towards the tree. It made a loud noise when it hit the trunk, but the boy paid no attention. Now she was sure he could not hear and apparently could not speak.

"I wonder if he works for Roger Hoelt," Nancy mused aloud.

"He probably does," Mrs Glick said. "Do you think we ought to tie him up in the carriage until our search is over? If we don't, I'm afraid he may run off and warn the man."

Nancy wondered about this. Nancy said that her chief concern now was to find Manda Kreutz and induce her to leave the Hoelts before she notified the police.

"Then we won't worry about this boy," said Mrs Glick. "Where do we go next?"

Before Nancy could make up her mind, she heard Bess calling to her. "Come quickly!" the girl urged.

"Where are you?" Nancy called back.

"In the wood near the house," Bess replied.

Nancy dashed off in the direction of Bess's voice, requesting the Glicks to watch the strange boy. When Nancy reached her friends she could hardly believe her eyes. Talking to George and Bess was a sweet-faced Amish girl—Manda Kreutz!

24

Caught!

"Manda!" Nancy cried excitedly, running up to the Amish girl. "I'm so glad that we've found you at last! Are you all right?"

"Yes," replied Manda, looking a little surprised. She went on to say that she was living with Mr and Mrs Roger Hoelt. "They are very nice people and are restoring this old house."

"Nice people!" George cried. "They're anything but that!"

Manda frowned, then asked George what she meant by this.

"You explain, Nancy," said George. "Bess and I haven't told Manda anything about the mystery."

After hearing the story, Manda was amazed. She could not believe it. The Hoelts had been very kind to her and were paying her good wages. Manda added that they were Church Amish from Ohio and spoke Pennsylvania Dutch very well.

"I do not see how Mr Hoelt could be a thief," she said stubbornly.

"Well, he is," George told her bluntly. "And the sooner you get out of here the better."

Sadly Manda hung her head, saying she had no place else to go. Her papa would not let her return home and she did not want to work in Lancaster.

Nancy smiled. "I've talked with your mother and father, Manda. They want you to come home. Your father regrets being so harsh and will be glad to have you back."

The Amish girl looked at Nancy as if this were not possible. Finally she said, "You speak the truth?"

Bess looked indignant. "Of course Nancy's telling the truth."

But Nancy did not blame Manda for not being completely persuaded, either that her family wanted her back or that Roger Hoelt was a thief. "I must convince her," Nancy thought, and said aloud, "Manda, have the Hoelts moved any furniture into the house?"

"Oh, yes."

"Beautiful antique furniture?" Nancy asked. "Are there one or more tables from George Washington's home?"

Manda looked startled. "You know this?"

Nancy gave her additional details of the mystery, and finally the Amish girl said she believed now that Mr Hoelt was indeed a thief. She would leave the Hoelts' employment immediately. But she did not want to report them to the police. "You will have to do that," she said to the young sleuth.

Suddenly Nancy recalled the boy who had been painting the hex sign on the witch tree and asked Manda who he was.

"He is a harmless boy who cannot hear or speak," the Amish girl answered. "Todd lives here too. Mr Hoelt writes out everything for him to do. Todd is not very smart, but he is a good worker."

"Did Mr Hoelt ask him to paint the symbol on the tree?" Nancy queried, telling of the strange way in which it was being done.

Manda nodded. Mr Hoelt had claimed it was a hex sign used by his family years before. He was very proud of it, and planned to have the hex sign painted on the barn and various other places when he restored the farm.

"He told Todd to paint the symbol on a tree but not to let anyone see him." Manda laughed. "The poor boy probably hid when he saw you coming but tried to go on with the painting."

The girls smiled, then Nancy asked Manda how she had located the farm. The Amish girl revealed that Mr Hoelt had not given her very clear directions when he had suggested she come to work for them.

"All he said was that the house was near the old *schnitz*. I could find it by looking for two witch trees."

"Is there really such a thing as a witch tree?" Bess asked. "We thought it was just a nickname for a tree with witches' broom growing on it."

"That is right," Manda replied. "I figured Mr Hoelt meant an old tree with *hex bayse* near the *schnitz*. I asked lots of people where the *schnitz* was, but nobody seemed to know. Then I met an old man on the road and he told me to come here. When I saw the witch trees, I knew this was the right place."

Suddenly Manda looked round her, a frightened expression coming over her face. She said all of them should leave at once.

"You mean before Mr and Mrs Hoelt catch us?" George put in.

"Not exactly," Manda replied. "But they will be back this evening. I want to be far away when they drive in."

The fact that the Hoelts were not at home pleased Nancy. This would give her a chance to make a positive identification of the furniture before reporting the Hoelts to the police.

"Please show us first where the antiques are," Nancy requested.

"All right. But we must hurry," Manda said, starting for the house.

Nancy walked beside her and asked the girl if she had ever heard of an old secret connected with the farm. Manda shook her head.

Nancy pursued the subject. "Manda, did you ever overhear the Hoelts say anything about a mystery connected with the place?"

Again Manda said no. Then Nancy asked her if she had

screamed while running in the woods near one of the smaller houses on the property.

Manda smiled. "Oh, that was Mrs Hoelt," she replied. "She saw a stray dog."

Manda was amazed to learn that the three girls had been so close to the farm such a short time before. When Nancy told her about the attic episode, Manda said this would account for Mr Hoelt coming into the house with his hair and clothes very dirty. He had said that he had been in the attic of a relative's house looking for an old family Bible which he had heard about the day before.

The Amish girl opened the rear door of the farmhouse. In the kitchen were just a few pots, pans, and dishes. Manda explained that the Hoelts, since they planned to redecorate the house completely, had brought in only four bunks and the antique furniture. The antiques had been stored in two attic storage rooms, because the painters would soon start work.

"Mr Hoelt told me never to mention the furniture because someone might try to steal it," Manda explained.

George said in disgust, "A clever cover-up."

"Shall we go upstairs now?" Manda asked.

"Yes," said Nancy. "I have a list with me of the furniture stolen from the Follett mansion in River Heights. I'll see if the pieces here seem to be the same ones."

The four girls climbed two flights of stairs to the attic. Here there was a centre hall with a window in the rear. A storage room opened off each side of the hall. Nancy noted the heavy Dutch doors, which had unusual locks. They were made of iron and were fully six inches square. From them protruded an enormous key with a loop on the end of each one as big as any of Nancy's bracelets.

Manda unlocked one of the doors. In the light from the hallway and from a small ventilator at the far end of the room, the girls could see several pieces of old furniture. Nancy went from one to another, eying them carefully. After looking them all over, she said:

"I'm sure these pieces came from Mrs Follett's home. But, Manda, none of the George Washington tables is here."

"They are across the hall," the girl replied. "Mr Hoelt said they were the most valuable and put the tables by themselves."

She unlocked the other storage room and the girls went inside. There were four George Washington tables! Nancy surmised that probably two of them were genuine, the other two were the copies Mr Zinn had made. So Roger Hoelt had found the valuable matching cherry table!

Nancy asked Manda if she knew where it had come from. "Mr Hoelt said he bought it in a New York antique shop."

"Well," she said, smiling, "our search is ended."

"I'm glad," Bess sighed. "You deserve a lot of credit, Nance, but it will be a relief to wind up this case."

"And I vote for that, too," said George, "although it has been a lot of fun. Congratulations, Nancy."

"I never could have done it alone," the young detective spoke up quickly.

Manda thought it was marvellous that Nancy had traced the stolen pieces. "And to think also that you fixed everything for me with Papa and Mama so I can go home. It would be wonderful to go now, ain't?"

"We'll start right away," said Nancy. "And we'll stop at the nearest farm with a telephone and call the police. They should be here to greet Mr and Mrs Hoelt when they arrive."

The girls were so absorbed in their discussion that no one but Nancy, out of the corner of her eye, saw the shadow that suddenly fell across the doorway. Whirling round, she caught a fleeting glimpse of a man who thundered, "You will never do that! You will die first!"

With this, he slammed the door and locked it!

"Mr Hoelt!" Manda cried out. "Let us out!" The reply was a mocking laugh from the other side of the barrier.

The girls leaped towards the door, pounding on it and trying to batter it down. At the top of her voice Manda cried out that Mr Hoelt had no right to lock her in. He must release all of them at once!

Her plea went unheeded. Then the girls heard Roger Hoelt hurrying down the stairway.

"We must get out and capture that thief!" Nancy cried with determination.

Together, the girls threw their weight against the door time after time, trying to break it down. Their efforts were futile.

"We're prisoners!" Bess wailed. "He's going to leave us here to die!"

25

SOS!

Frantic that they would suffocate in the hot, stuffy attic, the four girls continued their efforts to break down the locked door. But finally they were forced to give up, their shoulders bruised and sore.

Bess was on the verge of tears. In the darkness the others could hear her moan softly, "Nobody will ever find us here."

Nancy felt far from cheerful, but she tried to encourage her friends by saying that perhaps Mrs Glick and Henner would bring help,

"Oh, no, they won't!" Bess wailed. "That awful man has probably captured them too by this time!"

Manda had not uttered a word and Nancy asked her how she felt. "I am all right," the Amish girl said. "But it is my fault that all of us are trapped here. I should have known Mr Hoelt might return earlier, even though he told me evening. He rarely went anywhere in the daytime. He was always out at night."

Nancy persuaded the girl that she was not to blame. But the young detective too felt bad because she had been so close to capturing the thief, then had lost her chance.

George, practical as usual, pushed one of the tables to the wall directly under the ventilator. She climbed up to breathe in some fresh air and to investigate the ventilator as a means of escape. The bars were tightly built into the wall with three-inch spaces between them.

"No chance to get out this way," she said, "but if anybody feels faint, I suggest coming up here for a little air."

"Maybe we can use the ventilator for another purpose," said Nancy. "We can signal for help."

"With what?" asked Bess forlornly.

Manda remembered having seen a paraffin lamp in the room. "Is that what you had in mind, Nancy, using a light to signal with?"

"Yes, Manda. You're becoming a good detective."

The Amish girl found the lamp, then asked if anyone had a match. Nancy produced a box from her dress pocket. Matches and a flashlight were part of her detective equipment, but this time the flashlight was in her stolen car. She lit a match and Manda tested the lamp.

"It's all right and there's enough paraffin in it," the Amish girl stated.

"It won't do any good to signal until it's dark," Bess spoke up. "And by that time there's no telling what may happen to us."

To pass the time, Nancy decided to try locating the secret drawers in the genuine Washington tables. As she worked, Nancy told Manda the story. But after a half hour's search Nancy had not found the drawers.

"They're certainly well concealed," she said. Bess and George took turns but had no better luck. Suddenly Nancy had a new idea. If the secret drawers were so hard to find, it was possible that the gypsy woman had not known about them. If she had secreted a note in one of the tables, it might well be in some other part of it.

Nancy examined every inch of the two tables. Finally it occurred to her that one of the legs looked just a trifle different in length. When she measured it with the other three, using her arm as a ruler, she found the leg to be about one-sixteenth of an inch longer than the others.

Standing the table on its side, she began to wiggle the leg. After several tries she felt it loosen slightly. Excitedly Nancy twisted the leg and found that it actually unscrewed. In a moment she had it off.

Wedged inside was a small piece of paper!

By this time, the other girls had jumped to her side. As they watched in astonishment Nancy removed the note and read it, as George held the lamp.

Emil, My Beloved

Someday our paths will cross again, but now I must flee. Wherever I am, my love and thoughts will always be for you.

Before I leave, I want to warn you. Yesterday I learned the secret of your farm. I nearly stumbled into a deep hole located near a stand of oak trees—you know the place, for we have often met there. Had I been alone, I would have vanished like members of your family.

But my brother Gato rescued me. We wondered about the hole. He went down on a rope with a lantern and found a crystal cave. It is large and beautiful and someday will bring you riches.

I have planted bushes of wild flowers from the forest over the hole, so you will never fall in. This will prove my love for you. I beg you to leave your papa and find me.

Your loving gypsy,
Amaya

Speechless, the girls read and reread the note to themselves. At last they knew the secret of the old Hoelt farm!

"Roger Hoelt will return here someday and find this," Bess said dejectedly. "He will be a rich man and all of us will be dead!"

George chided her cousin for such melancholy thoughts. "We'll signal and get out of here yet!" she said with determination.

Fortunately, dusk came early. Nancy climbed on to the table top and held the lamp up to the ventilator. Passing one hand in front of the light at intervals, she gave the SOS signal. Over and over she repeated this until her arms were weary. George climbed up to relieve her, then Bess. They all knew the call. Manda marvelled at such efficiency.

"I hope someone sees it soon and understands," she said.

At this moment the girls, hearing heavy footsteps on the attic steps, caught their breath. Was Roger Hoelt returning with reinforcements? Would the girls be further harmed? Would he now be the possessor of the secret in the table and take advantage of it?

The key turned in the door. The girls stood together, ready to defend themselves. The door opened. To their relief, they saw two police officers in the doorway. They were State Police officers—Wagner and Schmidt.

"Oh, boy!" George cried out. "I never was more glad in my whole life to see anybody!"

"Were you giving an SOS signal?" Officer Wagner asked.

"Yes," said Nancy, and quickly told how they had been imprisoned by Hoelt. Then she showed the policeman the note about the crystal cave.

"I can hardly believe all this!" said Officer Wagner. "Nancy Drew, it is remarkable how you have solved this mystery."

"But it isn't completely solved," the girl detective replied. "We still have to find Mr and Mrs Hoelt." She said that possibly they were in her car which had been stolen.

"A very good deduction," said Officer Schmidt. "We haven't had any word that your convertible was picked up."

As the whole group hurried down the stairs and went outdoors, Nancy asked the policemen if they had seen Mrs Glick and her son Henner.

"No," Officer Wagner answered. "Are they here too?"

"I don't know," said Nancy, explaining that the Glicks had come to the *schnitz* with the girls but had stayed behind near the witch tree.

"They may be prisoners," she said. "We'd better go there and look."

They hurried along with the policemen who beamed their bright flashlights ahead. As they approached the witch tree,

the rays of light picked out the woman and her son, gagged
and bound to the tree trunk.

Quickly the two were released, then stories were exchanged.
Mrs Glick said that when Nancy had gone off she and
Henner had stayed behind to watch the deaf mute so he
could make no trouble. "But he got away just before
Mr and Mrs Hoelt drove in with Nancy's car," Mrs Glick
went on. "We tried to escape, but they caught us. They had
another man with them."

"I'll report all of this at once," said Officer Wagner. Over
his short-wave car radio, he sent a message to headquarters,
giving a full report and requesting that every road be
covered until Mr and Mrs Hoelt and their companion were
apprehended. Then he added:

"We'll take Nancy Drew and her friends home before we
return."

Mrs Glick wanted to take the horse and buggy, but the
officer suggested that she leave them until morning. They all
crowded into the officers' car, which was parked on one of
the little-used roads.

It was a long and bumpy drive back to the Glicks'. On the
way Nancy, who was sitting in front between the two
officers, asked what had brought them to the old Hoelt
homestead.

"You just didn't happen to be there to answer my signal,"
she said, a twinkle in her eye.

The officers confessed that they had been making a very
intensive investigation of Roger Hoelt. They had learned
about the family homestead and had decided to go there and
look round.

"You were just in the nick of time," Bess spoke up.
"I was nearly suffocated."

Officer Wagner smiled. "I'm glad we found you, but that
doesn't lessen the fact that it is Nancy Drew who has solved
this case."

Nancy made no comment. As always happened when she

had solved a mystery, she began to wonder what the next challenge would be. It was not long in coming, for at that very moment events were taking place that would enmesh the young detective in another exciting adventure, *The Moonstone Castle Mystery*.

The police officers kept their radio tuned in to headquarters during the entire drive. To everyone's elation, the news was flashed to them a little later that Mr and Mrs Hoelt and their accomplice had been arrested. They had been caught driving in Nancy's car, which would be returned to its owner at the Glick home.

The broadcast went on to say that Roger Hoelt had confessed to having posed as an Amish man from Ohio. In his childhood he had lived in Lancaster and had learned the customs and language of these people. Therefore, it had been easy for him to pose as one of them.

Hoelt admitted that when Nancy found out he had taken the Follett furniture he had tried in every way to keep her from locating him. He had resorted both to violence and to defamation of her character.

"The witch tree symbol was his undoing," the police officer announced on the short-wave radio. Hoelt had copied his family's old hex sign on a piece of paper and lost it at the Follett home when he stole the furniture. When he came back to look for it, Nancy and Mrs Tenney surprised him there and he had fled to the first floor. Hearing of Nancy's plan to search the house, he had run away and checked out of the hotel. Three days before this, he had made a phone call to his accomplice in Lancaster saying he was ready for the man to bring his truck and steal the antique furniture.

The evening of the day when Nancy had surprised him in the Follett mansion, Hoelt had planned to spy on the Drew home. While cruising back and forth in his car, he had seen a chance to hit Togo and had done this out of spite.

Later that evening he had phoned Mrs Tenney. Disguising his voice, he had posed as an antique dealer from New York and had cleverly induced Mrs Tenney to tell all she knew about Nancy's part in the case, including the fact that she was going to Lancaster to try to find the thief. Hearing this, Hoelt had at once started for Lancaster. On the way he had mailed the warning letter in Montville.

Hoelt on a trip back to Lancaster, after his release from prison, had heard about the secret in the old table. Since the secret was reputed to have some connection with the old Hoelt property, he had seen a chance of finding a treasure, acquiring the property cheaply, and then becoming wealthy.

From the time he had learned Nancy had taken the case, he had worked against her, trying to keep her from locating him.

"But he failed!" cried Manda, leaning forward to hug Nancy. "If you had not come to Amish country, I would not now be going home to my parents. Oh, I am so happy to have met a wonderful person like you!"

Nancy smiled and returned the compliment as Manda dropped her voice confidentially. "I will tell you three girls a secret," she said. "I met a fine young man in Lancaster who wants to marry me in a month. Papa and Mama will like him too, and I know they will give me a big wedding. Nancy, George, and Bess—you will promise to come, please?"

"We'd love to!" exclaimed Nancy as George said, "You couldn't keep us away."

"It sounds dreamy!" Bess said with delight. "And you Amish have wonderful wedding feasts"—she chuckled—"ain't?"

Nancy Drew®
Mystery Stories

by Carolyn Keene

Have you read all the books in this thrilling series?
Here are a few of the titles available:

The Clue in the Crossword Cipher (5)

Nancy travels to the mountains of Peru in search of priceless treasure. But she soon discovers that an unknown
enemy is determined to stop her . . .

The Whispering Statue (14)

The eerie statue of the Whispering Girl points Nancy to an
ancient mystery that haunts the decaying Old Estate. But
horror awaits her in the night . . .

The Triple Hoax (51)

An invitation to a display of magic puts Nancy on the
track of a ruthless gang of con men. But she soon realizes
that the tricksters are dangerous criminals . . .

The Silver Cobweb (65)

A mysterious spider symbol is Nancy's only clue to a jewel
robbery. But she quickly becomes enmeshed in a terrify-
ing web of danger . . .

Armada

Nancy Drew®
Ghost Stories
by Carolyn Keene

Six haunting mysteries

Nancy Drew is queen of the crime-busters, a girl with a gift for solving the unsolvable. But now she tackles dangers menacingly different from any she's faced before — spinechilling horror from beyond the grave . . .

The savage ghost hounds that haunt a lonely farmhouse . . . The phantom sailor who returns from the dead . . . The ancient gypsy curse that points to terrible tragedy . . .

Six eerie tales of mystery, intrigue and fear.

Dare you read them?

Armada

Here are just a few of the best-selling titles that Armada has to offer:

- ☐ The Beggar's Curse *Ann Cheetham* £1.25
- ☐ Cave-In *Franklin W. Dixon* £1.25
- ☐ Little Men *Louisa M. Alcott* £1.00
- ☐ The Boy Next Door *Enid Blyton* £1.25
- ☐ The Phantom of Dark Oaks *Ann Sheldon* £1.25
- ☐ Theodora and the Chalet School
  Elinor M. Brent-Dyer £1.25
- ☐ Heidi *Johanna Spyri* 95p
- ☐ Indiana Jones & the Temple of Doom Storybook £2.95
- ☐ The Spookster's Handbook *Peter Eldin* £1.25
- ☐ The Gateway of Doom *J. H. Brennan* £1.50

Armadas are available in bookshops and newsagents, but can also be ordered by post.

HOW TO ORDER
ARMADA BOOKS, Cash Sales Dept., GPO Box 29, Douglas, Isle of Man. British Isles. Please send purchase price plus 15p per book (maximum postal charge £3.00) Customers outside the UK also send purchase price plus 15p per book. Cheque, postal or money order — no currency.

NAME (Block letters) _____

ADDRESS _____

_____

_____

While every effort is made to keep prices low, it is sometimes necessary to increase prices on short notice. Armada Books reserve the right to show new retail prices on covers which may differ from those previously advertised in the text or elsewhere.